T0194322

Praise for *Sentimental, Heartbroken Rednecks*

"'Deep down we are all paupers,' Greg Bottoms writes. 'Some of us just insist on perpetuating the charade that we are not.' The power of *Sentimental, Heartbroken Rednecks*—which is considerable—derives from Bottoms's ability to unmask this charade for every person in the book, including, most especially and crucially and hearbreakingly, himself."
—David Shields

"A big talent that deserves a long run."
—*Boston Globe*

"Bottoms's prose is sparse and direct, imbued with a passion to write honestly and with sympathy for a people who might not otherwise have a voice."
—*San Francisco Chronicle* (Editor's Pick)

"Adeptly shifting between first and third person, Bottoms instantly engages readers with the honest and simple (but not uncomplicated) voices of his characters . . . Pain and sadness underlie the day-to-day activities of ordinary Southerners in these stories, but Bottoms is unafraid to let a few rays of hope breach the clouds in this sensitive and impressive fiction debut."
—*Publishers Weekly*

"Bottoms writes with a feverish intensity, depicting his many phantoms, dead and alive, with uncanny clarity. Each story is perfectly crafted, offering a first line that sets you up and a last line that knocks you out, with no wasted words in between . . . Highly recommended."
—*Library Journal*

"Serious and searching."
—*Washington Post Book World*

"Bottoms writes like a poet, creating characters who make his readers feel compelled to read more just so they can be a part of this dark intimacy."
—*Arkansas Democrat-Gazette*

"Greg Bottoms writes about people and places that Faulkner might have written about had Yoknapatawpa County been in the 'hood. The victims of fate who populate his inner cities are cut from the same cloth as those in the fictions of Denis Johnson and Raymond Carver in a particularly nasty mood."
—*Hartford Courant*

"[A] feverish debut story collection."
—*Chicago Tribune*

"There is far more heartbreak than sentimentality in this important young writer's second effort."
—*Austin Chronicle*

"In his strangely calm, assured voice, Bottoms stakes out the territory of his own unique style—volatile, intriguing, wild, mixing fiction and nonfiction in a manner reminiscent of Tim O'Brien. This is a highly promising debut collection of short stories."
—David Means

"It's hard to refrain from listing the writers who come to mind when reading *Sentimental, Heartbroken Rednecks,* for this superb story collection calls to mind the brutal honesty of Richard Ford, the psychological nimbleness of Harold Brodkey, the resilient faith of Andre Dubus. But Greg Bottoms possesses his own distinct, utterly convincing voice, and in *Sentimental, Heartbroken Rednecks* he creates a marvelous, disturbing world of mayhem and despair and the relentless pursuit of redemption."
—John Gregory Brown

Sentimental, Heartbroken Rednecks

Other books by Greg Bottoms

Angelhead: My Brother's Descent into Madness
The Colorful Apocalypse: Journeys in Outsider Art

Sentimental, Heartbroken Rednecks

STORIES FROM THE NEW SOUTH

GREG BOTTOMS

COUNTERPOINT
Berkeley, California

Portions of this book, in different form, first appeared in *Alaska Quarterly Review*, *Another Chicago Magazine*, *Boldtype*, *Brevity: A Journal of Concise Literary Nonfiction*, *Creative Nonfiction*, *Exquisite Corpse*, *Mississippi Review*, *Nerve*, *Poets & Writers*, *Prism International*, *Salon*, and *Witness*. "1967" was reprinted in *The Beacon Best of 1999*, edited by Ntozake Shange. "Patron Saint of Thrown-Away Things" appeared in Spanish translation in *Tameme: Nueva Literatura de Norte America*. It was also made into a radio documentary by the program "Soundprint," on Radio New Zealand. An abridged version was reprinted in *Utne Reader*.

Library of Congress Cataloging-in-Publication Data

Bottoms, Greg.
  Sentimental, heartbroken rednecks : stories from the new South / Greg Bottoms.
    p. cm.
  ISBN-13: 978-1-59376-130-1
  ISBN-10: 1-59376-130-9
  1. Southern States—Social life and customs—Fiction. I. Title.

PS3602.O88S46 2007
813'.6—dc22

                                                    2006038794

Cover by Kimberly Glyder Design
Interior by Megan Cooney
Printed in the United States of America

COUNTERPOINT
2560 Ninth Street, Suite 318
Berkeley, CA 94710

www.counterpointpress.com

I tried to save the world, but it didn't work out.

—Richard Selzer

Contents

I.

Nostalgia for Ghosts
(NOTES TOWARD A BEGINNING)

The dead are the imagination of the living.
—John Berger

A S A SMALL BOY, I suffered from extreme fevers. They came like phantoms, burning through me, blurring my vision. They covered me in cold sweat, ridding me of food and liquid and waste until I was aware—without the reserves of language or the ability to name my fears and feelings—of a new kind of existence, an emptiness and lightness of body.

The fevers always began accompanied by fear and anxiety—the same dread that animates dreams of falling—at times so forceful that I thought I would suffocate, dying on an old, worn-out couch or on the cold bathroom tile. Once my temperature settled, though, topping out at 103 or 104 degrees, there was a sickly ease holding me, as if I'd stepped into another world.

High temperatures came first from the croup: deep, painful coughs like lightning strikes at the solar plexus, threatening to split me in half. Later there were middle-ear infections: buzzings in my head, the outside world muffled through antihistamines and painkillers. Then came bronchitis: a tightening in the chest, a lack of oxygen, mucus rising like an organic sludge from the bottom of my lungs until every sound from me came wrapped in a bubbling wetness.

Some of my clearest memories, existing with a near-photographic clarity untrammeled by the erosive nature of time, are of my mother holding me through long winter nights over a steaming sink or bathtub as I stared blankly, dreamily, crazily at the dirt- and mold-spotted mortar between the tiles of the room. She would drape a towel over both our heads so that I would breathe only steam. In a sonorous, calming voice she would sing as we rocked, until, miraculously it seemed to me, she had saved me from dying again—a thirty-year-old heroine in a tattered robe and shaggy slippers, the purple half-moons of exhaustion, of complete parental depletion, weighing down her eyes—opening up my bronchi so that I could breathe, maybe even sleep.

In the morning we would be at the doctor's office again, where both the horror and the strange magic of sickness would be temporarily destroyed.

❖

I routinely saw ghosts during the heights of illness and fever. I stop on this memory. Surely it is false. But perhaps that is not the point—truth or falsity, fact or imagination. Whether the ghosts were figments or not, my visions of them, and my steadfast belief as a boy in the reality of these visions, were real, as truthful as anything I can think of, perhaps more so because of their force, the space they take up in my memory.

When the fevers came, I would lie nearly paralyzed by fatigue and a sort of slow-motion hysteria in my dark room in our small, brick house in Tidewater, Virginia. Crickets and frogs complained through the open windows. And I waited for shadows in the shape of the dead to walk through my bedroom door. Ghosts would stop, three paces in— always three paces: one, two, three—then vanish, each dark phantom becoming the next, like images bleeding together in a kaleidoscope.

On Sundays, my family would go to the Methodist Church near our home, often walking there along the edges of corn-fields, through a path in the woods, across vacant, overgrown lots. I didn't mind going to church then (though I stopped attending completely as a teenager, when I discovered alcohol and marijuana and what I thought of as the liberating sounds of the Sex Pistols and X, among others), because the stories of Christ and the apostles, of miracles and magic and the inexplicable, were usually interesting and well told by our minister.

One Sunday, after a long week of illness and fevers, dur-ing the season of Lent, when the church was filled with purple cloth and white flowers, I first heard, or first really listened to, the story of Christ rising from the dead. Though this was certainly the most intriguing story thus far at church, beating out even Job and his boils, or Moses parting the Red Sea or the burning bush, or Christ conjuring food and drink from virtually nothing to sate the hungry masses, what made it profound to me was that it explained the ghosts that I saw with every high fever. People, people who lived on the earth long ago or shortly ago, died, and were buried; but then, because Christ made it so, they rose from the dead and continued living, many of them for some reason stopping by my room.

To my mother sitting beside me in the pew I said, I can see people like Jesus.

She looked at me. What? she whispered.

In my bedroom sometimes. There are people like Jesus.

Sshh, she said, her hand resting heavily on my leg. Don't say things like that.

A young girlfriend, Debra, the person I spent most of my time with on the weekends and in the summer, lived three doors down in a brick one-story on a quarter-acre grass lot identical, almost, to my family's. She was adopted, as was her brother. Her father went jogging one day. He was forty, overweight. It was one of those heat waves you expect in the South—steaming asphalt, a weight to the sunlight, midday silences, mirages of water receding on the highways where the smell of melting rubber lingered. He had a heart attack on the sidewalk near my home. People came out, tried to help; paramedics were called. But it was too late. In a neighborhood where he had lived for nearly fifteen years, a neighborhood in which real estate values were plummeting because of enforced busing, racial unrest, and spiking crime rates against person and property, his heart had clenched tight and quit.

I saw it happen. Or I think I saw it happen. In my memory there is a space reserved for the image of his collapsing: he is tying his shoe, then putting his ear to the root-cracked concrete to listen closely to a faint rumbling underground, then lying down to rest, to sleep.

Weeks later, after the funeral and the still silence of mourning that engulfed their house, I told Debra not to worry, that death was a door. People were still around, and mostly fine, and sometimes, when I was sick, I could see them. I buttressed my story with talk of God and Jesus, of Mary Magdalene, of the giant stone rolled away, of the empty tomb, the triumphant light of holiness and salvation. I now knew a story that could make everything better. I believed that somehow made me powerful, impervious to life's ultimate tragedies.

Getting off the bus one day—I was seven— I watched as a girl in a wheelchair, with a miniature body and a normal, adult-sized head, made as if to cross the busy highway just outside of our subdivision, where the bus dropped off the neighborhood kids on the wide sidewalks. The day was hazy, steamed up around the edges like a televised dream. The girl couldn't see around the bus—a wall of yellow, the roar of cars. Probably she was mentally as well as physically impaired.

When the car hit her, she was thrown high into the air, coming down, lifeless, on the street's grass median. The bluntness of the moment was a shock, like a hammer to the face. There was something false about it. It lacked narrative, lacked the simple decency of making sense. It was nothing like TV. No swelling of triumphant or tragic music. No fog effects, or noirish shadows around the body, no commentators spouting irony or melodrama or some sophisticated mixture of both. No chalk lines to be drawn. No dissonant guitar chords, or quick cuts toward overly weighted symbols, or a darkening screen to pull it all together. I'd gotten used to death as it was presented by the experts, people who'd studied the science of human perceptions, who knew about narrative formulas and the mathematics of audience emotions. Now Debra's father and this—what?—midget? Dwarf? Death happened in the blink of an eye; then it was over, a life expelled—so simple as to seem degrading, the degradation so venal as to almost necessitate an afterlife.

The bus driver, a large woman with strange configurations of moles like stellar constellations on her face, sent all the kids away. Then there were cops, paramedics, a quickly forming crowd. Someone was shouting and shouting and shouting, but you couldn't understand any of it because the language was bent by panic, embroidered with loss, rising up and up and dissipating like factory smoke over our replicated houses.

At home, feeling numb and tingly, jarred and electrified, my spine fairly humming from adrenaline, still not quite believing what I saw to be real, I became sick, as if some tragedy virus had spread from the incident. I couldn't tell my mother what happened, not clearly anyway. I couldn't find the breath, the right words. She heard about it from Debra's mother. She tried to cheer me up, to make me forget, with promises of treats and cartoons.

I didn't go to school for the rest of the week, complaining, falsely, of an intense stomachache, staring blankly at cartoons all morning (Wile E. Coyote dying and coming back, dying and coming back), running errands in the afternoon with my mother—the beauty salon, the drugstore, the post office—seeing, on the periphery of my vision, the dead girl rising up in shop windows. I noticed people in wheelchairs everywhere. I suddenly lived in a city of deformities—something wrong with the air here, the water. I had a strange feeling that if I went back on the bus I would be sentenced to see something like that every day. I wondered if during the next fever the little girl, or tiny adult, would roll through my darkened doorway, the bent wheels of her chair squeaking and clanking.

But I did go back to school. Eventually I had to. My best friend there was a black boy named Barry Fox (I haven't even changed his name for this). He was the funniest, smartest kid I knew, a true comedian with timing well beyond his elementary years. He said things to kids like: *Your momma's*

*so fat she leaves a ring around the pool. Your momma's so
fat she has to butter the bathtub to turn over. Your momma's
ass got its own zip code.*

One Monday, early in the spring, Barry didn't come to
school. He didn't come on Tuesday or Wednesday either.
On Thursday he showed up again but didn't say anything.
Finally, at lunch, there was some talk that his nineteen-year-
old uncle, who lived with him and his mother and sisters in
the Pine Chapel "projects," had been stabbed to death in a
fight. I could tell he was about to cry.

Again, in an effort to console, I mentioned my power to
see the dead when I was sick. I tried to reassure him with my
devout Christian faith.

What the hell you sayin', he almost shouted. He was suddenly furious, telling me that I didn't know a thing about his
uncle, or about Jesus, or about his family, or about black
people, or about anything at all. He said that his dead-ass
uncle wouldn't be let into my white-ass house anyway, dead
or alive. He was right, though I did not understand the complexity of this at the time. Then he told me he hated me.
Then he did cry—I remember, or imagine—right into his
open hands.

I needed a fever to prove to myself that this was real, that I
could see what I thought, what I believed, I could see.

But it was spring, harder to get truly, deathly ill when the
weather was beautiful and warm. And—both blessing and

curse—I seemed to be getting heartier, healthier, outgrowing my sickly nature.

I would often go over to the Drabbles' house. They were strict Southern Baptists. The father was a mechanic, as mean and quick to violence as any man I have ever been around; the mother stayed home with the nine children, ranging in age from four to eighteen. The children were not allowed to swim; the boys could not wear short sleeves or short pants; the girls wore floor-length handmade dresses and were not allowed to cut their hair, ever, their astounding manes cascading down below their waists. My family lived cramped in our small house with only four. They lived in a house considerably smaller than ours with eleven, which meant things tended to spill outside.

What spilled out of the house were the beatings. The father would take the boys out and beat them with his fists, rubbing their faces down into the dirt of the yard. The girls he would beat with a leather belt as he swung them around the yard by their hair or shirt or arm, each girl screaming at a slightly different pitch.

Usually, though, Mr. Drabble was not home weekdays.

I went to the Drabbles' because they were, due to the pressures of their strict upbringing, I imagine, the worst kids I'd ever known—a whole new species of bad. The boys had pornographic magazines and shot BB guns at neighboring houses; they smoked cigarettes and drank stolen liquor in the woods. The oldest boy, who recently had a bullet shot into the door of his primer-colored El Camino "by a motherfucking spook," always had pot and an assortment of pills.

The other thing that spilled out of their existence into the yard, piling up in the backyard, was junk. A paradise of junk. Because the father was a mechanic, a poor mechanic, a do-it-yourselfer, a fixer-upper, he brought home old engines and minibikes and motorcycle parts and steering wheels and hood ornaments and tires and bent rims and smashed-in doors and washing machines and refrigerators and forklift parts.

One day, Rodney, the youngest boy, a boy who had learned much from his father, a boy I imagine is now in a penitentiary, began throwing heavy hubcaps into the air, seeing if he could accidentally smash one of his sisters' skulls. One came down onto my head and knocked me nearly unconscious. It sounded like an alarm went off in my brain.

Later, with my mother again tending to me, I felt nauseated, with, probably, a mild concussion, and I thought that perhaps a fever would follow. But, disappointingly, it didn't.

❖

A few weeks after this, on a blustery afternoon after a large northeaster had brushed the East Coast, taking out trees and light poles and local fishing piers, some kids and I were playing during a church social and cookout with an army parachute, the origin of which escapes me, but I imagine it had made its way from Vietnam into some kid's attic.

We devised a game. The wind was thunderous. The wind was an angry scream. You could let the parachute fill and it would tug several children holding on to the ropes along through a field, laughing and screaming.

The game was who could hold on the longest before the old parachute came to rest in a copse of trees. Being the winner of this game meant that I floated up over the field, up over the world, seeing broken bottles and abandoned tires and dog feces whizzing by beneath me, until, at a speed of ten or fifteen miles per hour, I would guess, I went slamming through saplings and ultimately into a large pine tree.

For a moment, the wind knocked out of me, I felt close to death. But I was seven, strangely able to shake off even the harshest physical traumas with nothing more than a good cry. I was eating Brunswick stew within the hour, singing Good News Bible hymns. *Man,* someone said.

When my mother was out of the kitchen I began sticking my head in the refrigerator, having heard that cold air on your head brought on sickness. I ate soap; I ate a whole can of years-old liverwurst I found in the back of my grandmother's pantry because I'd once thrown up after doing so on a dare. I tried eating my grandmother's chitlins (pig's large intestines, fried). Nothing.

Summer evaporated. Fall arrived, with the sad news that we would be moving to a much nicer place, where only solidly middle-class white people lived. My father, in that American cultural classic known as "white flight," was going to stretch himself financially to get us out of this neighborhood, this city, and this school district that he believed were crumbling all around us.

Our impending move, our "moving up" in the world, was devastating news. I needed the fevers to see the ghosts; I also, I believed, needed the exactly perfect darkness of my bedroom in the hissing silence of night.

❖

The first cold snap came with rain and wind. I was down the street at Debra's, who often asked me if I had seen her father. It wasn't for her, really, but for her mother, who no longer left the house, who just sat at the kitchen table in her bathrobe, drinking instant coffee, staring at the chipped Formica.

Rain tapped on the windows of Debra's room. Grayness coated everything.

I left their house and, through pouring rain and cold wind, walked across the fields near the church, out into the woods. I stayed there for several hours, praying. I didn't know how to pray then, not really, not in the way I would learn years later, when I was angry and unmoored and broken, but I gave it my best, most earnest try. I leaned against a tree in the weird bright darkness, shivering and soaked, asking God to make me sick, to make me almost dead, to show

me one more time that life was not just this, not just simply
this. I prayed until I heard my mother and father shouting, a
bit frantic-sounding, from our backyard.

Within forty-eight hours, I had the flu, a middle-ear ache,
and the beginnings of the most virulent case of bronchitis I
have ever suffered through.

My fever spiked at nearly 105 degrees before dropping
back to 102. I slept in an icy tub for an hour, dreaming of
carousels and lawn ornaments and ladders and wild cats and
my mother's voice miles and miles and miles away.

Night again. I remained still in my bed. My head throbbed
with every heartbeat. My mouth held the corroding taste of
sickness. The darkness was perfect. I waited for Debra's father, or Barry's uncle, or the miniature, deformed girl in the
squeaking and clanking wheelchair, or someone, anyone who
had died, ever. I stared into the blackness. I leaned forward.
Out my window, out in the real world—there *is* a real world;
I know that; I've just never been on great terms with it—a
car horn was bleating, and a dog was barking, and someone,
somewhere, was falling asleep.

1967

he himself grows in me we eat our defeats
we burst out laughing
when they say how little is needed
to be reconciled

    —Zbigniew Herbert, "Remembering My Father"

H ERE IS HOW I IMAGINE IT, how I might begin the
book of my father: with a vision of his mother, under a
mottled Virginia sky promising rain, gray rolling over bruise-
colored gray, faint streaks of yellow from the sun like a
healing outer edge. Their dilapidated house on a street
of dilapidated houses, all built in the thirties, during the
Depression, when, as the rest of the country suffered, southeast Virginia grew fat and strong around a shipbuilding
industry and military bases—the fear of fascism and com-
munism in Europe. A single chicken pecks hungrily in the
overgrown yard. It is 1967. The old house, like every house
on this short side street, has long since forgotten what

prosperity was like: wind whips through its seams; the roof sags like the spine of an aged horse. And a woman, old beyond her years, sits under the cracked and splintered porch eaves, dressed in a dirty pink nightgown, a single pale, sagging breast hanging lifelessly out of the material. She is drinking the heart out of a darkening fall afternoon. A group of young boys on bikes in the vacant street laugh, never taking their eyes from the pink, misshapen nipple. It sparkles like a coin to them. Occasionally these boys shoot BB guns at the woman from the woods. Because children are innocent and cruel. Because they haven't thought much about her—except to ponder her misshapen breasts. She is a redneck, they say, with their dirty faces and slow accents. She swats the BBs as if they are mosquitoes, gets a swatter to hold in her lap while she drinks, will later put calamine lotion over the welts that, oddly, don't itch. *Go to hell,* she would shout in this opening scene, taking a drink.

My father pulls his '65 Mustang, the best thing he has ever owned, into his mother's pocked driveway. It is three years before he is my father and twenty-six years before his funeral, where a great-uncle I barely know, almost weeping, gives me this story, the one that could serve as the beginning of a book, if I only had the patience and the strength, the memory and the nerve; it was, as he told it, a broken story in need of great repair, but also a good one, or so it seemed to me then, and it still trails me around. It was a backward story, the way he told it, an anti-tragedy, one that began with death and ended with life—a wishful story at a time when wishing seemed futile. And in this story, as it was told to me and as I might re-imagine it, my father stands in the overgrown yard, staring at the boys in the street, making eye contact with the leader, giving them his meanest look, which, I remember, was fairly tepid. The kids, like kids, ride off, shouting, *Your mom has nice tits!*

He is medium-built, my father, in 1967, with dark blue eyes and freckles. We're Scotch Irish. His hair is reddish brown and wavy, fashionably unkempt, and long, bushy sideburns reach past his earlobes. He's wearing brown velour. He likes Creedence Clearwater Revival and The Who. He is unconventionally handsome, I think, in the few pictures I still have of him. He looks at his mother, his eyes moving immediately to her sagging breast, white as a new golf ball. Jesus, he thinks, not as prayer but as lament. His father, her husband, has recently died, at the age of fifty, of a heart attack, and his mother, who has been drinking like this for years, has now been drunk for several straight weeks. Soon she will wreck a new car bought with insurance money; later, before she is put into a psychiatric ward, she will catch the house on fire by letting a cigarette fall from her whisky-wet lips.

My father and his father barely spoke, just as my father and I, at times, will barely speak. My father loved his father, though, in a quiet, obligatory way. They never hugged, generally kept their distance, but they would have fought for each other, broken a pool cue over someone's head for each other. It was that kind of love. You are a boy and then you become a man. You learn what parts of yourself to hide. He made his father's funeral arrangements, spent all of his money on the service, and still, as of fall 1967, owes some.

Something about my father's father: When my father decided he would return to high school after dropping out for two years, the old man resented him, called him "uppity." He made fun of high school, talked of the righteousness of hard work with your hands and your back. He had been a migrant farmer as a boy, had worked hard and long, then spent years as a laborer, going where the work was, until he quit all of that toward the end of his life for some ill-advised moneymaking ventures: a flop of a grocery store in a bad part of town, a pig farm that put them deep into debt. On my father's graduation day, 1962, as students two years younger than he huddled with their families for pictures and sang songs and then went off to celebrate, my father walked sullenly to a friend's house, where several high school dropouts sat around drinking beer and watching baseball on an old TV. During the ceremony—the speeches and congratulations—my father's father was sitting on a bench in

front of the gas station, staring at the traffic; his mother was
passed out in her bedroom. That night my father got drunk
and never mentioned the ceremony, which was, after all,
just a ceremony.

Now, in this story, the one the great-uncle told me, my father
walks up the drive toward the small house. His mother sees
him but says nothing. He loves his mother, too, but the love
feels like an obligation, sometimes a curse. It is an exhausting
sort of love. He thinks, and will always think until his death,
that love is often more work than it deserves. He has come
out here several times this month, to find her sleeping in the
woods, sleeping with the oven on, sleeping in a neighbor's
front yard at night with the group of boys around her, laughing. He imagined the boys pissing on her and chased them.
He imagined the urine dripping off of her forehead, her eye-
lashes, as she smiled in a dead sleep. To the neighbors, the
scene must have been both sad and comical: the neighborhood drunk slumped half dead in the yard, her half-crazy
son chasing the boys again. The western sky, he notices, is
the color of the veins in her legs. Her circulation is poor. Her
blood is thinned by alcohol, her heart pumps slowly. Mr.
Purcell, a neighbor, a kind old pipe fitter for NASA, called
about the stink: I reckon a coon or a big old black snake got
up under the house and died. It smells something awful over
there. The phone call alarmed my father. He remembered the
last call about the smell.

❖

Sometimes my father dreams of his father, as I will dream
of him. Dreams are like the best books, I sometimes think:
they tell you things you may not want to hear; they chal-
lenge you to think something, feel something; they make you
uncomfortable, because every dream, no matter what it is
about, is about the dreamer. In dreams, my father pushes
his father's head down a hole in the street; his father shoots
his mother for wildly fucking another man while drunk;
his father gargles soup at the rusty-legged, linoleum-topped
kitchen table—that's it, just leans his head back and audi-
bly, almost musically, gargles soup; my father finds himself
along the shores of the Chesapeake Bay, walking the beach,
searching for his father's eyes like fiddler crabs so he can put
his father back together—everything depends on finding his
father's eyes, which are nowhere to be found.

❖

The stink.

❖

Something else that should go into this book I'm not going
to write: Once, not long before his death, my father's father
drove my father's old car off of a bridge. The bridge was
new. You could look through police records and see that he
was the first person to get a car to go off of that bridge.

People scratched their heads over this; it pointed out a design flaw. Cars weren't supposed to just go sailing into the bay. A sailor from Norfolk—this is true—jumped off the bridge and saved him. It was in the paper. It was like something from a movie—if you focused on the heroism of the sailor rather than all the complicated stuff about the victim. The logical question is: Did he try to commit suicide or was this simply an accident? It's unclear. The answers are lost to history. But he never thanked the sailor. And he never apologized to my father for crashing his car, which, as far as I know, is still on the sandy bottom of the bay.

About that earlier scene: My father tucks his mother's breast in and she pays no attention. It is oddly cold in his hand. Her face is gaunt, collapsing, eyes as yellow as a healthy boy's urine. But she remarks with lucidity about the weather as she stares out at the thick, wet distance, says how it will be too rough to fish later, as if it were possible for her to fish later without doing her own falling off of bridges. So he would sit on the bench beside his mother, surely he would do this, put his head in his hands, sigh—a practiced gesture.

His mother and father were separated at the time of his father's death. She was in the hospital having a procedure done for an ulcer (they performed surgery on them back then).

My father got a call from the cops. They had found his father three days after he'd died of a heart attack. My father had to go to the house, sign some papers, answer some questions, identify, verify. It was still hot then. You can imagine. The body was swollen. The skin was gray. Eyes open. It was as if he'd drowned, a delayed reaction to driving off of the bridge. Maybe he'd been dead for a long time, my father might have thought, and had waited to lie down in darkness and start stinking to let everyone know. His dog, Henry, a terrier mutt, was lying still beside the body, ready to go out. Henry had been hiding under the bed when the cops came in earlier. The dog perked up its ears, wagged its tail when my father opened the door. My father ejected disbelief into his open hands, instinctively trying to avoid making a mess in his father's house.

Something about my father's mother: My father had a pet rabbit as a boy, a little white one named Bugs, and one day his mother told him to go get it. She was sober. He handed it to her with complete trust. He was maybe ten, eleven, not yet cynical, wary. He understood nothing of alcoholism, madness, suicide. All of that was later, still too early for a boy, but later. She broke the rabbit's neck with her bare hands. It screamed. Rabbits can scream like wounded babies. When he cried and refused to eat Bugs, his father said, Fine, more for me. On this fall day in 1967, he thinks of this when the smell hits him, even, oddly, before he thinks of his father's swollen, gray body. He can't believe she can sit here, no matter how drunk, in this smell.

She keeps drinking and talking of fishing, of blue skies, of the time they went, just the two of them, right after they were married, down to Florida, to the Gulf Coast. Blue water and huge colorful fish. These words could be anything: baby talk, the grocery list, another fishing story. She is unraveling, tiptoeing toward breakdown. She doesn't look at my father. She goes on. He (my father's father) caught one so big that they grilled it and fed everyone at the hotel. They were heroes for a day. They smoked cigars in the sun. They were wearing new clothes. They both had jobs back in Virginia. It was a beautiful day. They had coleslaw and big hunks of exotic fish. Her nightgown opens again. She doesn't notice, or simply doesn't care, he can't tell. She tries to conjure other good days, furrows her brow at the chicken pecking in the yard. She drinks from a tall, chipped tea glass. My father walks into the house to get a flashlight so that he can get under the house and see what's dead. He takes a bandana from his pocket, one of those red paisley ones, and puts it over his face, tying it behind his head like Billy the Kid. He feels like a boy.

The smell of death sends him reeling, thinking of the rabbit, his father's swollen body. The luck of this house. He had

aspirations of playing major-league baseball, of living far
from all of this. He'd gone out West with the national cham-
pionship all-star baseball team from Virginia, 1960, and the
sky, just like he'd heard, was enormous, limitless, not like in
the South, where it was low and wet a lot of the time, even
when it was sunny, reminding you always of the boundaries of
your life. The West—Montana, Colorado, Utah—that space,
that vast American emptiness, made his heart grow big in his
chest, made his scalp tingle with possibility. Growing up he
sometimes felt like a speck on the sad, wet earth. The shouting and the drinking and the occasional tossing of dishes had
closed in around him like walls. Instead of getting tough, he
became overly sensitive, moody, lacking confidence in everything from school to girls, everything but his ability to hit and
field a ball. And then he ruined his knee, just kidding around
with dropouts, playing basketball in a pair of slippery loaf-
ers. The injury kept him out of Vietnam, sure, but it also kept
him out of baseball; it kept him away from what he imagined
was his only chance to live out in the open, free.

❖

But he did find ways. He kept his head above water; he didn't
go driving off of a bridge.

❖

He rifles through drawers, looking for the flashlight. We are
back in the opening scene of the imaginary book. The smell

is strong, maybe too strong to be under the house. He can't find the flashlight. After hurting his knee, after the doctors told him it would never be right again, my father was depressed. He was stuck in his life as it was. He ran his father's grocery store after dropping out of school. It was when the store went under that he returned to school and graduated. Then he took care of his father's pig farm, something his father bought before he died, thinking it would make money. It didn't. He sold all the pigs to slaughter after his father's death—for a loss, but good riddance. Soon he would work in a bank. Then, finally, by 1970, the year I was born, he'd take a job at the Newport News Shipyard, this when he'd conceded that he would never fulfill his dreams and that he needed to imagine new things to dream.

But on this particular day, he is unemployed.

It's not under the house. It's Henry, my father's father's dog. That's the big twist, the O. Henry moment in imaginary chapter one. Dead in the bedroom, on the bed. Dead for a while, a few days. Jesus, my father thinks, not as prayer but as lament, what is it with this? How do these things go unnoticed? The dog has *collapsed*. Dead for a week or more. He thinks Henry may have starved, barked and whined and panicked until he finally lay down to sleep, but then pushes the thought away. Heart attack. Old age. Easier. Neater. He picks up Henry and thinks of the rabbit, his father, and now his mother out on the porch and those boys who go into the woods to shoot BBs at her, who stand around her when she's drunk and dare each other. If he were not himself, he thinks, looking at the stinking dog, and he were instead one of those boys, one of those boys with their whole futures in front of them to ruin, he'd probably do the same thing. He imagines shooting BBs at his mother, standing over her in the yard, in the dark, daring himself and the boys to degrade her, to demolish her, his mamma, his first love.

Here is how bad my father's luck—and by genealogical extension my own luck, my family's luck—was. He eventually died, almost twenty-six years to the day from the dog incident, of malignant mesothelioma caused by asbestos fibers, which he got while working for more than two decades at the Newport News Shipyard. That may seem too lachrymose, too contrived, to even put in a book. When I think of this, his illness, I think of baseball, of his knee, of dead rabbits and dogs and fathers, of dreams and dead dreams and dreams of death as ordered and uncomfortable as a good book, of the fact that his father and mother wouldn't take one fucking afternoon, a couple of hours, to go stand in a crowd for what was perhaps a pointless ceremony, a ridiculous American ritual, while my father graduated from high school at almost twenty years old (only slightly older than I was when I received a bachelor's degree, for which my father—who embarrassed me a little, who was such a man from the underclass—went out and spent more money than he should have on a camcorder to capture my pointless ceremony, which he made sure I knew was anything but pointless), which was one of the most difficult things he ever accomplished, which is why I'm writing these notes for chapter one without the words "grandmother" and "grandfather."

Something about me, the narrator, the non–book writer: In college, for a time, I read Eastern philosophy (I might have grown a goatee if my face would have cooperated). Then I read Hesse and Kerouac and Huxley and D. H. Lawrence's ramblings from Italy and Taos, New Mexico. All that unencumbered ranting. All that love and suffering. Those books were about me. I wanted to be that sad happy tragicomic narrator bleeding that jazzy blues-filled bebop prose, a dirty reefer-stoked martyr for the lost and the never-quite-made-its who considered myself no more or less important than anyone or anything else. One can incorporate, attribute, luck to the karmic wheel, to *samsara,* the endless cycle of birth, suffering, death, rebirth. To yin and yang, to universal equanimity, to positive and negative sharing equal space, et cetera. Nothing has to *mean,* it just *is.* One can have a clean mind and body and a stoic understanding of tragedy, if trained properly, if ascetic. But I failed in every way. I am about as capable of following religious dogma as a dead mutt (dead

for a week, let's say, starved to death by its drunken owner)
is of winning the blue ribbon in a dog show.

After college, I moved to Richmond, a couple of hours up the
James River from where I was born. My father was dying. I
tried not to think about it; it became all I thought about. I had
four jobs that year and quit them all. I fancied myself some
kind of poet—part Robert Lowell, part John Berryman. I was
filled with what I thought of as the necessary angst and tur-
moil; I was willing, in that Judeo-Christian way, to confess;
I just lacked talent. I read all the time. I wanted the Western
fucking canon to save me. I drank all the time. I wanted hops
and barley to save me. I was frightened of my father's death
as if it were my own. I rarely went home to see him, to stare
into my own face, instead calling him, having incredibly positive, superficial conversations while he had trouble breathing. Distance, I hoped, would alleviate the obligation of love.
It didn't, like I knew it wouldn't, like he knew it wouldn't. I
was a coward. On the morning of the day my father would
die, my younger brother called. He was sixteen and stayed
home with my father, getting him to the bathroom, wiping
his mouth. He was crying. He couldn't even talk, but I knew.
I was broke. Like my father, like my grandfather, money
eluded me; it seemed I wasn't supposed to have it. I didn't
have money for gas to get home. I took quarters out of a
jar in my roommate's room. All the signs along the highway
were blank and I floated unmoored through timeless space

without touching the accelerator or the steering wheel or hearing the radio that was on full volume. Two hours later, when I reached my house, there was a sign that said OXYGEN IN USE: NO SMOKING. I was stuck. I didn't want to go in. I thought, for just a second, about leaving. Inside, my father was in bed. The cancer had spread to his liver; his poisoned blood was pumping through his body. He was wearing a diaper. He weighed eighty pounds, having lost half of his body weight in less than a year, a third of that in the month since I'd seen him. I barely recognized him. He was fifty-one. I was twenty-two. I've erased a lot of this. There were many moments and I don't want to get to know them again. But I remember lying in the bed with him, both of us staring at the rough, white ceiling, still shy about showing affection, even then. Even then. You are a boy and then you become a man. You learn what parts of yourself to hide. I don't remember what was said, but he seemed to be listening, his legs slowly writhing like things under water. Less than two hours after I'd returned home, he died. I'd swear he waited for me, that he insisted on doing me that favor. My mother, my younger brother, and I stayed in the room with him. In the bed with him. Had it been my choice, at that moment, I might have washed him and kept him for three more days.

But about the dog and my father's mother, about *the dramatic action* of this story: The old great-uncle from North Carolina—a "public school administrator and a good,

God-fearing man," I was told—back at my family's house, the two of us drinking, eating ridiculously small biscuits from a tray. He finished the story. He wasn't a good storyteller. He backtracked, said, No, wait, said, And then. He let the story veer all over the place, let the action stop dead in spots for some familial or historical commentary. Then he'd pick it back up only to do it again. It was a story and a history and a confessional and an elegy and a complaint and a prayer. You might say *he tossed form out the window* and laid it all out there, this messy human thing. My father's mother had had a nervous breakdown. She never noticed the dog. She went into a hospital that year and saw her dead brother's face in a large plant. She told the plant how her "nerves was bad" and how much she missed him, how she was alone now and things weren't working out. Then she got better, not great, but better. She couldn't touch booze ever again. The couple of times she did were disastrous. And my father, said the great-uncle, that dark fall day in 1967, walked out the back door, the stinking dead dog in his arms, the bandana over his face, to avoid having his fragile mother see. And that was a part of it. The point. The message, the moral. He wanted me to understand the kindness in that gesture. She was still talking to the chicken in the overgrown yard. The boys were in the street, on their bikes, drinking sodas, eating candy. My father buried Henry in the woods, digging the hole with his bare hands.

❖

After the funeral and the reception (or whatever you call the non-party after funerals), after everyone had left, and my family was asleep, I was still drinking under a single lamp in the otherwise dark house, thinking about the story, picturing my father in 1967, thinking that he looked a little like George Jones back then, a little like John Fogerty. I was mulling it over, storing it up. The story connected to other stories, stretching back through time, springing forward through my life, my future, even far beyond me, until I was only a character in someone's story.

LSD in Raleigh

Under these circumstances there was no question of loneliness.

—Walter Benjamin, "Hashish in Marseilles"

ONCE SPENT TWO DAYS ON LSD. This was in Raleigh, North Carolina, in 1991. I was twenty. It was during the first Lollapalooza festival put on by Perry Farrell and headlined by his band, Jane's Addiction, the finest art-rock band, I used to say back then, since Ziggy Stardust and the Spiders from Mars or the New York Dolls.

I took three hits of acid, total. A girl with mustard-smelling fingers whose name I cannot remember softly placed the first small, square piece of paper on my tongue. We were standing in a cheap motel room that smelled faintly of old smoke and foreign bodies, of sex and something sweetly medicinal. I took the second hit that night while pacing alone around a parking lot between a Denny's and a Howard Johnson's, overly intrigued by how the humidity turned the high streetlights into glowing orbs the exact size of the moon, how the rain glazed cars in a Vaseline sheen, and how the bright neon orange of the Howard Johnson's sign was the gaping mouth of a volcano. I took the third hit the morning of the festival, while standing in front of a steel, water-spotted bathroom mirror in a Wilco gas station, staring at the intricate hair patterns in my eyebrows.

That day the world glowed, became an endless halo quivering with new meanings. My body was filled with hot helium. Gravity showed me a kindness and mercy I didn't know it had. Pretense was flayed away from each thing and person. Self-consciousness was a hundred pounds of chain mail I hadn't known I was wearing.

But I can't write about it, about the day, about tripping. I mean, *really* write about it. I can't capture the essence of the thing itself, the experience. I'm left with representation, symbols, metaphors, similes, words that hold some poetic or intellectual cultural associations that I can attempt to arrange in such a way that might evoke some semblance of how I felt. But it's bullshit; it's approximation.

There is a reason why writing about drugs, from Baudelaire to Burroughs and beyond, almost always, even in the most capable literary hands, trundles off into the familiarly banal, the cliché. There is a gap, a chasm, between raw experience and representation, most especially in regard to narcosis—but, frankly, in regard to everything. Our resources—language and the philosophy implicit within it—are limited. It's like trying to talk about God, or love, or psychic pain without sounding like a fool.

The English philosopher C. D. Broad (professor of moral philosophy, Trinity College, Cambridge, from 1933 to 1953, interested in the "scientific evidence for survival after death") once wrote, "the function of the brain and nervous system . . . is in the main eliminative and not productive. Each person is at each moment capable of remembering all that has ever happened to him and of perceiving everything that is happening everywhere in the universe. The function of the brain and nervous system is to protect us from being overwhelmed and confused by this mass of largely useless and irrelevant knowledge, by shutting out most of what we should otherwise perceive or remember at any moment, and leaving only that very small and special selection which is likely to be practically useful."

The insane, the tripping, and, I suppose, the visionary lose this "protective" or "eliminative" function. You step outside the world of symbols, out beyond the boundaries of what can, even in the most stable circumstances, *be* represented, and this, I believe, is why so much writing about the hallucinogenic experience quakes with the emptily reverential, faux spiritual, and bad poetry: the task, this task, is impossible. So here I go.

❖

The world that day, having changed none in makeup but enormously in meaning, suddenly seemed infinitely bigger. Schopenhauer's famous *The World as Will and Idea,* which I had just read in a college course, implicitly touches on this sentiment: The world is not the world but simply our experience of the world. William Blake wrote the famous line (giving name to both a band and a book): "If the doors of perception were cleansed every thing would appear to man as it is, infinite." Aldous Huxley, starting with Blake's sentiment, wrote: "That which, in the language of religion, is called 'this world' is the universe of reduced awareness, expressed, and, as it were, petrified by language." Huxley (because he was a writer) goes on to point out that both art and religion would be obsolete if we could live according to Blake's sentiment: "Art, I suppose, is only for beginners, or else for those resolute dead-enders, who have made up their minds to be content with the ersatz of Suchness, with symbols rather than with what they signify, with the elegantly composed recipe in lieu of actual dinner." What I realized on three hits of acid, as the world flooded in and out of me, nearly stealing my breath, was how pitifully small my thoughts and feelings had always been.

At the time, and ironically (since I was taking drugs with some gusto), I was starting to see—meaning, *think about in some slightly complex way*—the "horrors of drugs," how they had been thoroughly separated from any of that sixties'

idealism, how they ruined people's lives, how my own life hovered in a kind of limbo because of them, how the insular yet expansive universe of drugs in suburban America where I lived was one of constant lies and cruelly absurd occurrences, how kids I knew got locked up for a bag of coke or mushrooms or speed or crank or pot, or hung themselves in a shed, or got their girlfriends pregnant and denied it, or called up their old girlfriend and fired a shotgun into the ceiling of their tattered apartment (paid for by their parents) so she'd think it was a suicide, or decided to stand on the hood of a Jeep going sixty on a dark, desolate road, and so on and so on.

There are so many examples, so many things I was thinking about, obsessed with, back then, when I put all of that acid on my tongue. There was the impossible situation with my family. There was the kid who overdosed on heroin in his friend's game room (later found by the friend's father, an air force officer); or the one who held up an Applebee's in Greenville, North Carolina, with a toy gun, which he decided to do, the story went, to pay off pot debts (this was later featured on a short-lived reality-TV program hosted by William Shatner; I remember the ending of the segment showing the young man shouting, "This one's for you, Dad" into the camera. I thought, *Wow, I used to get high with him*). Or there was the guy, who used to hang out with my brother before his mental illness became too severe for relationships of any kind, who stole his mother's VCR and hocked it for a rock of crack; or the kid named Jason, with whom I once stole a bunch of stuff from a neighbor's house for no better

reason than simply to see if we could do it, who gave his car
to a huge black guy for drugs (I can only imagine the lie he
told his father, standing at a pay phone in a black ghetto in
Newport News, Virginia, with no car, shaking as the high
wore off).

I had spent the six weeks before Lollapalooza driving
around the country with money I'd made working construction, a low-grade sadness coursing through me like a virus,
sleeping in national forests in Idaho, Colorado, Montana,
and Utah, bathing in rivers, doing the young bohemian thing
as I vaguely understood and imagined it, reading what I figured were the underground classics—drug narratives, mostly:
De Quincey, Kerouac, Brautigan—I needed to have commit-
ted to memory.

Now, here I was in Raleigh, tripping, with a head full of
books and more than a little anxiety and melancholy over the
state of basically everything—my life and the lives spinning
out of control all around me.

There were thousands and thousands of people there, the music was blasting—Siouxsie & the Banshees, Nine Inch Nails,
Living Colour, N.W.A. ("Fuck the Police" was a big hit at
the time), Jesus & Mary Chain, the Butthole Surfers, Jane's
Addiction—but I was off by myself, wandering around the
Hardee's Amphitheater, into it, into all the beautiful minu-
tiae that were newly important to me, yet I was strangely outside of the event itself, outside of social norms, even outside

of the governing structures of time. I was lost not so much in north-central North Carolina as inside of my own skull.

The amphitheater was like a big shallow-grade pit with seats in it, the stage down at the bottom; around the pit/seats, in the back, was a long, green grassy hill. Because in my state I couldn't hang out with any of my drug friends—sadly lingering relationships from high school based upon all sorts of erroneous things—or focus on anything but my own thoughts and the interesting stimuli around me—an orange tent rope, a nipple ring, a squashed grasshopper near a paper cup with chewing tobacco spit in it, the rise and fall of some black-painted toenails coming toward me—I went to the top of the hill and started flipping down it.

I won't try to unravel the complex series of impulses and feelings ("thoughts" would be the wrong word) that brought me to this action because it would be impossible. But people cheered me on, probably with a little maliciousness, a little schadenfreude, in their hearts, hoping they might see me go away in one of the ambulances parked near the exits, as many would that day.

Go, motherfucker.

Yeah, man.

Get it, freak.

And of course I knew that these people thought I was insane, thought, probably, that I was, as I was, out of my mind, but I didn't care, because suddenly the gaze of others, as they say in graduate school seminars, really didn't bother me at all. I felt sorry for them because they didn't understand how important this was, how there was a perfect sync

to my movements, how I understood things about the grass
and myself and movement and energy that they, sadly, would
never, ever understand. I began humming an electrical tune I
felt mostly in my lips and throat. My eyeballs felt to be about
the size of elementary school classroom globes.

When sober I've always worried, been a little petrified,
about what people might think about me, if they think I'm
smart or cool or funny or ugly or handsome, I'm always on
some level *performing*, but not today, not at all; I was rolling
rolling rolling, flipping flipping flipping, and then getting up
at the bottom of the hill, which was seventy-five steep yards,
and throwing my hands up and laughing—the spectacle, the
freak, the schizophrenic off his meds—overcome with the joy
of flipping, as unself-conscious as I was when I was a little
boy and my mother used to sit in a lawn chair in front of our
little brick house and watch me roll through the grass singing
because I was flooded with life, the great, painful gift that is
life, totally consumed by the moment but at the same time not
at all aware that I was consumed by the moment (a prerequi-
site for being consumed by the moment). This part of the day
was like that part of childhood, early on, when you're getting
the first glimmers of what will become adult consciousness
and reasoning, when everything, the wide universe, has the
ability to astonish, to delight or horrify, and each moment
offers the possibility of something entirely new.

After flipping, I started doing long laps around the amphitheater, walking quickly with just shorts and sandals and
sunglasses on, not panicked but needing to move move move.
If I stopped for even a second I felt a strange, mystical wind

at my back. The sun blazed down on me. The crowds were made not of people but of colors and shapes.

Everything, all prior meaning, even at the most basic level, was gone. No, not gone, exactly—*subsumed* into something much larger and scarier but also far more delicate and beautiful. The world was vast and different. The insignificant—a white spot on the fingernail of a vendor—was vital, worth what felt like hours of my mind's energy (though it may have been only seconds). That which was vital in the straight world—my being cool, striking some practiced pose I was barely conscious of—was now so trivial, so small and confining, that it didn't even register. Who cared about music and grooving with your friends when there were these . . . *brick patterns that signified the perfection of nature, the existence of a loving God* . . . Or when the huge screen behind the stage was actually made of . . . *little blinking colored squares that were exactly attuned to every feeling in the range of human emotions present here today,* moving and changing at an amazing speed, proving, once and for all, that there was such a thing as *humanity*—I mean, you know, like we were one big organism, man, each one of us just tiny cells intricately, inextricably connected.

The floodgates, the eliminative or protective mental narrowing functions, were gone in a dangerous way. I was out beyond the limits of language—and not in any intellectual, poststructuralist kind of way; I mean I was *slobbering*—where thoughts and feelings were no longer separate things evoking each other but in fact the same thing coming in at higher, stronger frequencies.

I was only in this most intense state for a couple of hours. Then I started, slowly, to come down, to ease my way back into the familiar workings of the world. I was still extremely affected by the drug, but I at least remembered who and where I was, had some battered sense of ego creeping around, like a big wet worm, inside me.

There was a lot of political stuff going on, I remember, tents and booths all around the venue's perimeter, so now I went and got pamphlets about women's rights and tortured people in Third World countries and how technological progress was being perpetrated on the backs of Mother Earth and the poor, but the whole time I was thinking that there was no issue but love, which sounds ridiculous now as I say it—cliché drug-speak of the first order—but when I thought it then it was as tight and logical and true as a complex math problem finally solved. The grand answers to everything were this basic. Environmental problems—love! Torture—love! Oppression, repression, cruelty, emptiness, lies—love! I asked a meaty fraternity guy, the one person I might choose to hate for no good reason in that crowd, if he would hug me. And he did while all his friends laughed and shouted, *Faggots!*

Later I looked around and saw people dancing and singing, moving their heads, throwing their hands up. At the height of this I had been more aware of movement and mass, particular parts as opposed to whole human beings, but now I was more here, aware in a more conventional way. It was communal and perfect, and I was now also more aware of tripping itself. Like Benjamin in his hashish experiments, I was taking note.

I had a feeling that I was presiding over all this. For an instant, I thought I might go out and preach, as I have seen a few mentally ill homeless people do, from the gospel of kindness I had glowing inside me. *Look at the bricks,* I would say, *and the colors, and know, children, that God is here with us.*

❖

The sun and clocks were telling different stories, and this—how can I explain it?—began to bring on the first pangs of a spiritual dread. I tried to hide, but I wasn't sure from what. Then I got stuck in the bathroom.

You can imagine how a bathroom would look at a Lollapalooza Festival. There were people getting high, vomit and watery feces and urine on the floor and walls. But none of this bothered me. What did bother me—the urine feeling electric coming out of me, like long, solid, charged strings being yanked from inside of me by an unseen force—what got me stuck, were all the cigarette butts. Then I started thinking about the person who had to clean up. In my mind, it wasn't a squadron of cleaning people; it was just one little woman who walked around with a bucket—a bucket of sorrow, a bucket of shame. I began to weep. I did. Cigarette butts made me so sad. They were so *representative.*

Standing in front of the urinal, I became obsessed with this woman, this imaginary, symbolic, oppressed woman, whose job it was to clean all this mess up, and how she probably wasn't capable of handling a job this big. Where were the pamphlets, the mass mailings, and the booths for this woman, I wanted to know. Who would start the custodial revolution? Who would speak for the single anguished soul?

With tears abseiling down my cheeks, I looked over at the guy next to me and said: *Hey, someone has to clean this up so try to be careful with your spray and pubic hairs.*

I felt that pubic hairs, in particular, were cruel things to subject this lone woman to, a woman who now, in my mind, had just left an abusive husband and had five, no, *six* hungry children to feed, all somehow under the age of three.

He stared at me for a few seconds and then nodded. I was red and sweaty, and I hadn't showered in a couple of days. He might have slugged me had I not been crying, looking like a heartbroken serial killer.

❖

The day changed. The light changed. The tone changed. It was still good, still beautiful in a whole new way, with everything opened up to me for what it really was—or so I was convinced—but I was coming down fast now.

Night was falling. The sky couldn't totally darken because of all the stadium lights. Jane's Addiction came onstage. I went up to the top of the hill again, where the steep grass met the concrete, to watch.

I didn't know where any of the people I came with were. Perry Farrell brought out two women dressed in S-and-M outfits, and they were rubbing on him in a choreographed way, and the music was getting faster and faster, and he was shouting about Ted Bundy and fucking and the lies and exploitation of the media, and I was sweating still and feeling a little faint, a hunger moving through me.

Suddenly there was a guy with long hair and wearing a T-shirt with a pithy beer/sex double entendre. He asked if I was all right and I replied that I was—why wouldn't I be?—not realizing for the moment that he had pulled me up off of the ground, where I had been lying passed out.

When it was all over I was completely and utterly lost. I started getting a little worried about my friends then, thinking that they might have left me, that they might have seen me lapping the stadium with my giant eyes and my foul stench and become scared of me. I walked down the hill toward the gate and the parking lot, the muscles in my back and legs beginning to hurt from the earlier flipping.

As I said, before the trip I had been thinking about all the ruin around me, family problems, all the kids I knew who were getting busted, wrecking cars, becoming different, desperate people all of a sudden (that was a big part of why I went driving, rather aimlessly, around the country). Now these thoughts resurfaced, stronger than ever. And when I looked around after the show, my head roaring from the long day of loud music—the intensity of feeling from the height of the trip still lingering, but not a thing good about it anymore—I started noticing people, kids, lying in their own puke, or a big guy getting all over a sixteen-year-old girl on a towel who was just seconds from passing out, or two guys pushing each other, their faces close together, their mouths open, barking like feral dogs.

There was no epiphany, no bright holy light, no real moment of wonder. Just the feeling that I was in need of an ending. I wiped my eyes and tried to remember where we had parked.

Sam at the Gun Show

THE KID I STAND NEXT TO at the gun show and ask
about pistols—which ones he likes, what he'd buy if he
could, if he were eighteen—starts telling me about firecrackers. I've been watching him buzz all around the place, table to
table, picking up guns, putting them down, visibly annoying
some of the vendors. He's maybe sixteen, with a smattering
of cystic acne along his jaw and neck, big red carbuncles that
make me remember the almost suffocating embarrassment
I felt over my own bad skin when I was his age. He wears
baggy jeans and a yellow parka zipped up to the neck (an attempt to hide his bad skin, I think). His hair is down over his
eyes, black, shiny, almost wet-looking.

We're at Expoland, a giant "for rent" warehouse a
few miles from my home in the Blue Ridge Mountains of
Virginia, a place that hosts everything from quilting fairs
and livestock auctions to Christian revivals. It's 8:00 AM. I
walked here through the gray morning, over fields, along a

gravel road, breathing mist. I don't own guns and don't plan to buy any. But I like to walk when it's quiet; I'm curious; and there was a sign—"Biggest Gun Show of the Year"—so I paid five bucks to the old man in camouflage at the front door to see what exactly a gun show was like. The place, approximately the size of half a football field, with maybe thirty- or forty-foot-high ceilings, is nearly empty—twenty or thirty vendors, maybe fifteen men (all white) drinking coffee from Styrofoam cups and browsing. And then there's this kid. His name is Sam.

I don't know how he and I arrived at the firecracker story. There was no getting here, no one-idea-leading-to-the-next. He's just talking because I asked him something and I seemed willing to listen.

He says that, one time, when he was ten, his grandfather, who owns a farm near here, wouldn't let him ride the four-wheelers that everybody else, everybody older, got to ride. He was too small, his grandfather said, and the four-wheeler would roll over on him in some far field, over some distant rise, and they'd find him broken or dead. All of his cousins and brothers were there on this day. It was the Fourth of July. It was a big party. A bonfire was blazing because they had a bunch of trash they needed to burn. Anyway, everybody was taking turns riding the four-wheelers except him and his little baby cousin. He got "real real mad, you know," and he wanted to show his grandfather that he wasn't any damn baby. So he took all of the firecrackers they were going to set off in a few hours after dinner, a whole "shitload of firecrackers"—maybe a hundred different kinds—and he

threw them, all of them, into the bonfire. They started shooting all over the place, up into the sky and toward the house
and the big barn and out over the fields and some of them
shot straight out of the fire at face-level, like bullets or something. Everybody was ducking and screaming and "freaking
the fuck out," and he loved it, loved watching it, because it
was so funny and he'd gotten their attention. He was sorry
that some hay in the barn caught fire, sure. And he was sorry
that his older brother, Donald, beat him nearly senseless right
there in the dirt and no one tried to stop it, but other than
these minor things this seems to be a fond memory for him, a
defining personal myth.

His eyes are distant, drugged-looking.

Do you have any guns? I ask.

Shit, he says. I got like four guns—two hunting rifles and
two pistols. My brother's here somewhere and he's going to
buy another pistol, a Glock. Then he'll probably give me one
of his old guns for my birthday or something. People give
me my guns. I'd like to have that gun—he points to a $550
antique Smith & Wesson—but I ain't got no $550.

He sees his brother, a plump blond guy in a goatee and
wearing a football jersey, and walks away without saying
anything, shrinking across the room like someone's future
nightmare.

Strangers and Dreams

EVERY YEAR OR SO my boyhood friend, Sammy, re-
turns from the dead to speak to me. I wake up loose
inside of my skin, dry-mouthed. I say, *Oh come on;* I think,
the stubbornness of this dream!

I sit up, blink in the dark gray air. I'm damp in the sheets,
shaken, sentenced to stay awake for the rest of the night,
thinking of death, of the echoes from the past that vibrate,
shaking us along the way, through the present.

Refrigerator humming in the next room.

Street light outside.

Red numbers on the clock: 2:58; or 3:12; or 4:06.

Small, black-cornered room with the cracked-open closet
(broken doorknob) where my wife and son and I all sleep.

It is *now,* I remind the night, remind the breath of my
sleeping son and wife, and Sammy is still long dead.

❖

Sleeplessness, a doctor once said, peering down his nose through his small lenses, is an agony made worse if fought against, like a too-deep splinter. *Fighting* sleeplessness *causes* sleeplessness. The trick is "to relax"—the opposite of "to fight." So when this happens—when this *dream* happens, when Sammy comes floating back—I quietly get up and walk out of the bedroom. I lie on the futon. If it's winter, I pull a tattered blue and burgundy afghan around myself, the one my cat uses to sharpen her claws when left alone.

I read under a dim lamp, yellow-white dust motes between my face and the book: Edmond Gosse, or Thomas Merton, or Virginia Woolf.

Or I watch old movies, paying no attention.

Or I simply lie in darkness, away from my wife and son, afraid that my ill feelings from the dream might be contagious.

I wonder about his death—in the dark, in the night stretched tight around me.

The shooter, Lisa, said in court that he was going to rape her younger sister, Teresa, who was thirteen.

Sammy's friends—two boys who were my friends, too, all those many lifetimes ago—said she just walked into the laundry room where Sammy was standing and shot him in the temple, throwing his head back, a paintbrush flick of blood fanning across the brown-egg-colored washing machine and dryer, speckling a pair of blue and yellow Nike running shoes.

I can believe both versions, hers and my old friends'.

Maybe everyone was trying to be honest.

Maybe the bullet has gone through Sammy's head a thousand times in all of our dreams, each time bringing forth a tiny piece of the truth.

But let me go back, slide backwards into my room, past the crib, into the bed, next to my wife, under the covers. Adjust my head on the pillow. Shut my eyes. Sleep. Dream.

Sammy, fifteen, the age he was when he stopped existing in 1985, floats up out of the water of the river near our childhood homes in Tidewater, Virginia, where as boys we used to swim and fish, up over the end of a crooked, cracked, weather-scarred dock the color of parched driftwood, bone-dry from years of summer sun. The sky is concrete, the water slate, the patchy, small islands in the distance, fogged-over, half-hidden.

He wears old, too-big Levi's and a T-shirt with the sleeves cut off. His face is pale gray; black-purple bruises have formed half-circles under his eyes—something to do (in the dream) with where the bullet hit him and how his corpse rested in the funeral home.

He rises up not like an angel, or Christ, or some other magical, mystical presence, but like someone mocking these things, a punk rock blasphemer, and it makes me uncomfortable that he is still doing this, being disrespectful, even in death.

I get the feeling (in the dream) that I used to get when we'd be in a crowded mall, or at the arcade, two wild kids standing in line for the latest horror flick or teen comedy, and Sammy would start doing his "black" voice; or when he would hear something ridiculous at school and start pumping his fist in mock-masturbation, rolling his eyes for the fake orgasm. I want him to stop all the floating and the slight, tender, faux-angelic glowing and come down onto the dock before some-one in authority—who might that be?—sees what he's doing.

He floats down, his face coming close to my face (I am suddenly in my boyhood bed, and Sammy is hovering over me, horizontally, in my boyhood room), to tell me that I'm going to die. Then he tells me that there is a God (actually, he says "there is God," a strange syntactical construction that seems somehow meaningful in the midst of all this glowing and floating), but that he wouldn't know how to begin to explain what that actually means. He says it's not at all what you might think.

I go home. I do. Every once in a while I leave the college where I talk about books, where I say, "The force of Emerson's thought," or, "The truth is not one thing," and visit my mother. Even though sometimes in that city of my childhood I have to turn myself sideways or stand in a corner to avoid being trampled by a memory.

Back home, I walk around thinking (which, if depicted visually, would look very much like staring at air). I think things like: That is the house where Mark lived before his mother left and then he and his father left and he went God-knows-where; that's where Scotty's parents died of cancer and he started coming undone; that's the pine-scented house where Dan's mother, a Southern Baptist who claimed to have been "tested" by a demon sent to her bedroom, said we were all going to hell; we drove 105 miles per hour on that narrow road; Derek killed a ten-pound seagull with a fat stick in those woods, the poor thing begging for its life like a tortured prisoner; that's where the puddle of blood was after the fight, where the girl didn't love me, where my father and I banished each other finally with nothing more than declaratives worthy of Hemingway, where Lee flipped the car and killed Syd, where the kid looked at me and said, "What's *he* doing here?," where I passed out drunk and some older kids, kids I wanted to be like, pissed in my face and in my mouth for a joke, where Lisa put a bullet in Sammy's brain . . . This is all maudlin, I know—I shouldn't even be writing this—and my childhood was not without joy and wonder, certainly not without love and connection, but what I'm talking about is how the ache of a dream—or a fragment of memory—can shrink the distance between then and now, between the comfort of the present moment and a discordant note from the past. I'm saying that you *can* go home again, that at some point you will probably have to, that you can walk into the past, into memory—which is maybe like a dream, or maybe like a musty attic—and have every corpse you know come scratching out of its grave.

❖

For instance: I'm putting gas in my truck at a gas station. I'm visiting my mom for the holidays. This is a decade ago. I'm in graduate school. Or between graduate schools. I don't have a son; I'm not married, though I am in love. Gray out. Breath visible. I'm wearing a suede coat my mom bought me for Christmas. It's got a biker-jacket cut, with the short collar. In the window reflection, let's face it, I look cool.

Hometown. Shopping center, strip mall, fast food, pharmacy. Glance around, notice, don't notice. And here is Sammy's father. Beside me, putting gas in his pickup. Maybe this is time travel: running into people and things that seem to belong *elsewhere* and *before*.

I feel a coldness.

I stare out at the foggy traffic.

There is a scuff on my shoe, some cigarette butts, that tire there might need air.

Hey, says a voice.

Hi, Mr. R. Wow. How are you? How's . . . everything?

He stares at me as if I'm a ghost. His eyes are glassy. He stares and he stares. His son would be my age. His son would be a man. He's much heavier, puffy-faced. It's been years; it's been a few lifetimes. He reaches out to shake my hand, and as our palms touch, as his meaty hand squeezes tight around mine (for he is the type of man to squeeze a little harder than you), I speed back through time to Sammy's wake—where all the kids stood around thinking that this wasn't quite like the wakes they had seen in movies, where the light was a little softer, where the kids had bigger sorrow and fewer blemishes, where the dialogue had direction and dramatic purpose, where there wasn't all this dead air and waiting in line— where Mr. R. squeezed my hand, just as he is doing now, and told me to be strong and to keep my head up and to buck up and to keep my head up and to buck up and to keep my head up and to buck up and to keep my head up and to buck up and to keep my . . .

And it is all I can do, in this town of stunted childhoods and small catastrophes, in this moment halfway between then and now, halfway between the death of my friend in the past and dreaming of him in the future, not to let my head drop off and roll down the street, as if in a . . .

Mr. R and I smile and wish each other well. We are just two men putting gas in our pickups at the same time, saying hello. We part without mentioning the dead boy between us, the trial, the talk of rape, the shooter getting off, the newspaper articles, the tears of a mother, families destroyed, all the rumors, all the stories, that cling to this landscape like humidity.

We consider our silence courtesy. We're strangers, after all. I can only imagine his dreams.

Heroism

I WAS PARKED IN A VACANT CITY LOT, sleeping in a company truck, when the giant homeless man stuck his head inside of my open passenger-side window.

I worked as a legal courier, generally messing up the preferred whereabouts of vital contracts and documents. I'd smile at secretaries in important-looking offices—the kind with regal portraits on the walls and real hardwood floors and paneling and soft classical music piped in from hidden speakers—right before they said things like, *Oh, this isn't us, honey, this is the other firm, the one across town.* I was always floating around, thinking about some masterpiece I was going to write, my mind worked over by the ten-hour days and the driving and the thick diesel fumes and the unblinking sunlight. My incompetence startled even me.

Hey, said the man, his face eclipsing the sun.

I sat up, flung open my eyes, and let out a little scream that had been crouching in my throat for weeks.

I went to high school over there, he said, pointing out at the city. He said this with the soft, raspy intonation someone more mentally stable might use to say, *I am in love.*

Oh, I said, calmer now, thinking that he would simply ask me for change. That's interesting, I said.

Several of his teeth were gone. Shatters of blood vessels spread across his meaty nose. One eye was half shut. There was either dirt or a big grayish birthmark on one cheek.

He had been a star athlete in high school, the one out there in the ether that he kept pointing to. That seemed to be the gist of what he was saying.

Eventually, he asked me for a ride. The radio, the one they used to chastise me for botching deliveries or taking too long, wasn't barking any commands. I said, Sure, get in.

He smelled, frankly, like he'd soiled his pants a week or so ago and hadn't bothered himself about it. His belly nearly hit the dash. I think the spot on his face was a birthmark. Or cancer.

Where do you live? I asked.

Down there, he pointed.

I followed the direction of his finger. Where? I asked.

Down there, he pointed again.

He was pointing to an alley entrance strewn with garbage cans on the other side of the vacant lot. It was about fifty feet away.

That's where you live?

Yeah. For now. I'm looking around, though.

You want me to give you a ride over there?

Please. You'd be saving my life, man. I can't walk across
the lot with the sun like this, and all those weeds, man, growing up through the cracks. I'm stranded.

You're *stranded?*

Isn't that obvious? Look around you, man. I mean, just
take a look! Christ!

His face quivered like water. There was something loose
about it. He seemed like he might cry. I couldn't take that, him
crying in my truck. I felt a little quivery myself at the time.

I rolled over to the other side of the lot, near the alley,
at about five miles per hour. He tensed up, cringing, as we
rolled over the sunniest part of the asphalt.

He got out. He thanked me over and over, as if I'd given
him one of my organs, or a few pints of blood. I rolled back
over to the other side of the lot and tried to nap again until
the next call, which could be an hour or more around lunch-
time. I sat up to look a few times to find him standing there
in the shade, mumbling to himself.

Over the next six months, until I was getting ready to go
to graduate school, every time the man saw me pull into the lot
to nap with my radio hissing pickups and drop-offs, he would
waddle out of his alley, just to the edge where building shadow
met sunlight, and fling up his hands in victory signs, as if I
were some great hero returning home, as if I'd actually saved
his life by giving him a ride across fifty feet of hot asphalt.

Needless to say, I was having a hard time back then. I'd
lost a lot lately. My loneliness resided in the dead middle of
me, like starvation. I'd drive miles out of my way to see that
homeless man; to fall asleep, on the clock, a hero.

Heroism #2

I N FRONT OF BASILIQUE DE FOURVIÈRE, up in the
sky, my face moist from the cold mist moving, I saw the
whole city of Lyon, France, spread out in front of me, squat
geometric shapes of brown and white and gray. I watched the
specks that were speeding cars on a distant highway. I saw
the Rhone fat and muddy and red, like an artery.

The church sits atop the highest peak in the city. Its
old stone is the color of wet sand; its giant, weathered
wooden doors are as thick as a man. People—especially
Catholics—come here from all over the world. From the
top a green-blue statue of the Virgin Mary peers down at
the slow smallness of things. I studied the stone demon and
angel carvings outside.

Inside, there were scenes from the New Testament on
every wall: the virgin birth, John the Baptist's head, the
Last Supper, the Crucifixion, the Resurrection. You could
rub your fingers gently across any of it—across Jesus's baby

belly, through Mary's hair—and no one said a thing, and nothing in the world changed. High ceilings, arches, pigeons in the rafters bombing shit onto the pews, light spilling almost liquid—the whole tableau, I imagined, growing out of someone's dream of Heaven. Only it was dirty now, and wet, and smelled of mildew.

The day I went up, walked up and up and up, I was listening to Neil Young on my Walkman. I was hungover. The sky was a new bruise, painful. I had felt, until then, lost in France, a walking cliché—the poor American writer abroad!—with all the power of an infant, drifting in a foreign language, every sign a mystery, every gesture written in code. A few days before, after being scolded by an old woman in a state-issued janitor's getup, I finally figured out that I had to pay five francs to take a piss at the Eiffel Tower. An Algerian kid had nearly attacked me for my Levi's, the 501s I was wearing, on the Paris underground (he seemed to think I had stolen them from him or someone he knew, but of course I didn't understand a word of what he yelled at me). And I had left my copy of Orwell's *Down and Out in Paris and London* in the Louvre bathroom, where I spent most of a morning after a cheap breakfast of espresso and undercooked eggs.

Anyway—this is what I want to remember—when I came out of the church that day, I saw a homeless man playing an old, scratched guitar on the steps. He was filthy, wearing a jacket matted with something sticky—maybe whisky or red wine. He had a blond beard up to his eyes, down to his shirt collar, a little bald patch like a monk's on the top of his head. Tourists moved past him on the cobblestones—English,

Japanese, German, American; carrying cameras and back-
packs and babies—talking and pointing at the stained glass,
the intricate stonework, the ecstatic angels within reach.

I took off my headphones. The homeless man was singing Neil Young's "Pocahontas" in French. He and Neil
were almost on the same verse! I felt awake. I felt enlivened
and blessed. For a flash I imagined he had read my mind. I
was lonely, and missing things, we were at a church with
the Virgin Mary above us, looking down on us, the whole
rest of the world below, two lost souls at the top of the
hill, all of Europe, all of Western history, out *there,* both
of us thinking, almost unbelievably—come *on,* I thought,
this is unbe*liev*able—of Neil Young and Pocahontas and the
strange beauties and tragedies of America on the other side
of the Atlantic.

Neil Young, I said, pointing to the headphones around
my neck, poking at my heart.

Neil Young, he said in broken English, gesturing toward
the money in his open guitar case.

What heavenly glory in a moment of connection! The
sun came out. Rainbows curled over the land. The French
stopped speeding. The carved angels were black backup
singers, and Japanese tourists with space-age cameras took
pictures of them swaying. The meek were invited to sleep
out of the cold, and to use the restroom without charge.
What could I do: I gave Monsieur Young a piece of paper
that was some denomination of French money. He smiled
then—smiled big—so I might have been as generous as I'd
like to remember.

II.

Patron Saint of Thrown-Away Things
(AN ESSAY ON DEVOTION)

1.

St. James didn't think of himself as an artist. His in-
tentions went far beyond art. He didn't think of himself as a
"folk" or an "outsider" or a "grass roots" or a "visionary"
artist. He didn't consider himself any of the things scholars
have called him since his death in 1964. He didn't even know
what those names meant, not in the way they used them,
anyway. "Folk"? That's what he called his people down in
Elloree, South Carolina, where his sister sat on a splintered
porch thanking Jesus for the daylight, where the farmland
stretched right out to the hem of the sky, where "The Best
Pork Bar-B-Que in the World" was made out behind the
Stop-'n'-Go. And "outsider"? Man, that one was easy: every
nigger in America.

When he began *The Throne of the Third Heaven of
the Nations Millennium General Assembly*, a 180-piece

sculpture made from the refuse of a dying world, in that old rented garage in northwest Washington, D.C., where poverty could beat your soul into some new shape, where a man might rather put a bullet into you than shake your hand, he never would have imagined that one day it would be displayed in a museum, under fancy lighting, against a backdrop of majestic purple, where a janitor—a janitor just like him—would come by at night to dust it.

He built *The Throne* to prepare the world for the End Time, the Second Coming of Jesus Christ, our Savior, as prophesied in Revelation. He worked nights in various government buildings in the District, mopping floors and singing hymns from his childhood in Elloree, where he first saw the face of God when he was just a boy—not a shadow falling down in a comer or something smoldering at the edge of vision, not a feeling tickling in his spine or cloaking him in the Spirit's heat, but the *real face of God*—shining there in front of him one night like an explosion on a drive-in movie screen. It was at that moment that he knew he was chosen, knew he was a saint, knew that he had been granted life to serve God.

2.

James Hampton, Jr., arrived in his family's shack in Elloree in 1909, slick and shiny with birth, face aimed skyward, screaming like a true Southern Baptist. He was named after his father, a gospel singer and self-proclaimed Baptist preacher who would later abandon his family (a wife and four children, including James) in the early 1920s to travel through the rural South and preach.

In 1928, at the age of nineteen, after a childhood of farm work and family and strict religion, James moved to Washington, D.C., to join his older brother, Lee. The city was a new world—bigger, yet somehow claustrophobic, harsher, but beautiful, too—with the great monuments of America rising up into the sky, almost as if they somehow grew right out of the ghetto James and his brother lived in.

For more than a decade, James worked as a short-order cook in various diners around the city, keeping to himself, hearing faint voices, taking prayer breaks instead of smoke breaks when he took a break at all. At the end of a twelve- or fourteen-hour day, he walked home, slope-backed and exhausted; past men sleeping in alleys and boys hanging out on corners like packs of young wolves; past prostitutes saying, *Hey, little man, hey, Jesus, what I got make you see angels, baby.* He kept his eyes aimed at the ground—cigarettes, bottle caps, a bullet.

He wore his day home with him in a cloud of stink: old vegetables, coffee, meat, grease, garbage. And he could still hear the echoes of clanking dishes and order bells, even in the half-still city night, and somewhere down below all the noise of the world ringing in his head—always ringing in his head—he heard the faint mutterings of God like his own teeth grinding, like his own pulse. He'd shower in the apartment he and Lee shared, read his favorite passages from the Bible—Genesis, the Gospel of John, and Revelation—and sleep the sleep made of hard work. Then he'd get up and do it all over again. Day after day. Month after month. Year after year. The noisy world in his head. And underneath the noise, just underneath it, God.

3.

In early 1942, everything changed. James was drafted. He knew it was coming as soon he heard about Pearl Harbor on the night of December 7, 1941, right while he was squeezing the grease out of a pink, sizzling burger. Nigger like him, healthy and living in a part of the city white people didn't even drive through, he knew. But it was okay, too, a part of God's plan for him. He was a supplicant in the palm of the Father. He was thirty-three now, the same age as Jesus when they nailed him up in sunlight, and he was ready to sacrifice himself if that's what God wanted.

From 1942 to 1945, James served in the army's non-combatant 385th Aviation Squadron in Texas, and later in Seattle, Hawaii, Saipan, and Guam. His unit specialized in carpentry and maintenance, and James made (critics speculate) his first piece of *The Throne,* a small, winged object ornately decorated with foil, in 1945 on the island of Guam. He returned to Washington in 1946, after receiving a Bronze Star Medal and an honorable discharge. He rented a room in a boarding house not far from his brother's apartment. Then he found work with the General Services Administration as a janitor, not good work, but better than he would have gotten without that Bronze Star Medal and veteran status.

After a brief illness, his brother Lee died suddenly in 1948. He went to work one day feeling a little down, a bad taste in his mouth and sweat breaking out all over him—he hadn't been to a doctor in years because who could afford a doctor?—then came home, went to sleep, and never opened his eyes. They must have buried Lee down in Elloree on a bright, sunny Saturday, James reading a stitched-together elegy made of Bible passages over the grave, tears rolling down his face; the whole town gathered around, dressed up black as crows, softly singing hymns. But it was a short visit. After mourning and celebrating the ascendant soul of Lee for a day or two, James got on a train and headed back to Washington, sitting in the rear car, the "black" car, the Southern countryside smearing by in his window. Lee wasn't simply James's brother, he was his best friend, maybe his only friend, and now James, alone but not lonely because he knew all things were a part of His plan, began spending all his time envisioning *The Throne*. Lee and his janitorial job were his only anchors to this world. Now Lee was gone.

Back in Washington, he went out only to work, find materials for *The Throne,* and attend a number of different churches in the city (he didn't believe God would allow for strict denominations and divisiveness concerning His word). By 1949, at the age of forty, he felt the power of God buzzing electrically up his spine. The End Time was coming. He had sensed it during the war, in the stories he heard about what men were capable of doing to one another; he could see it now in the hard faces that hovered along sidewalks, could watch it growing in the people like a malignancy. It was both a curse and a blessing that he sensed it so acutely, felt the world's decay as a dull ache in his bones.

Some days now the low, gray sky would fill up his skull like cotton and he'd forget everything but God, forget who and where he was, and it was beautiful, this kind of forgetting, but then he'd come to on the street, walking stiff as always, General Services Administration uniform tight and clean around his small frame, and he suddenly had this *clarity,* he could see despair like a blanket of living, breathing fog over the streets. It was all he could do not to crumble as he headed to work those days, where he cleaned the floors and toilets of the people who ruled the world.

4.

In 1950, answering the request God had made in a dream, he rented an abandoned garage at 1133 N Street, N.W., from a local merchant, telling him he was working on something that required more space than he had. The garage was down an alley, out of sight from passersby, on a block more dangerous even than his own. It was dark and dusty, with brick walls, concrete floor, and light bulbs dangling from wires that traveled along creaky ceiling support beams. Rats scurried in the alley, darting between Dumpsters. Spiderwebs formed misty veils over comers. It was awful. It was perfect. It was exactly where God wanted *The Throne* to be.

Over the next fourteen years, James found a routine. He worked until midnight, mopping floors and picking up trash in government buildings, then went to the garage to do his real work for five or six hours, listening closely to what God was telling him, finally going home to sleep when the first pink light of dawn started creeping up the Washington Monument.

Some afternoons and many weekends, he would visit local used furniture stores, rubbing his hand across coffee tables, feeling how sturdy the leg of a chair was, staring for long minutes at a rickety old chest, then asking about prices in a voice just above a whisper. If he liked something, he'd return later with a child's wagon and a pocketful of folded-over dollar bills soft and worn as tissue paper. He carted away things that had the merchants scratching their heads: legless tables, drawer-less desks, half-crushed dollhouses, leaning stools.

Later, you might have seen him walking from a government building with a trash bag full of used light bulbs; or maybe out on the street with a croaker sack, asking bums if he could buy the foil off of their wine bottles. He'd dig through Dumpsters to get green glass, sandwich foil, cardboard. And of course the best thing about working for the American government was how wasteful they were, throwing out perfectly good material because they didn't like the way it looked. Sometimes he'd even get brand-new stuff because someone ordered twice what was actually needed. It made him smile, these finds. The best thing about cleaning up after the people who ruled the world was that they didn't see the real value in things.

5.

Occasionally, after long hours of work, after a face full of government cleaning chemicals and toxic solvents, his brains felt like Jell-O bumping up against his skull, and bits of time disappeared like old pennies. But other days everything was sharp and sensible. On these days of clarity, James . . . *St.* James turned into God's lightning rod, a cipher for the Word.

He had grown up with the Bible. Bible was his first language. He could remember his father preaching in Elloree, sweat on his forehead like a field of blisters, people standing around in the backyard *testifying*. *Praise God!* He knew the power of God before he had any inkling of Self, knew later that there was no worthy Self without Him. But when he had these days of clarity, of *vision,* that's when he knew the world was ignoring God and His commandments, knew the End Time was near. Six million Jews, *God's chosen people,* exterminated. He could barely get his head around that one. And in his own neighborhood, a murder every day. Stealing. Lying. Coveting another man's woman like it was some kind of game. The list of human cruelties would take you a million lifetimes to recite.

So St. James wrote ten new commandments for the world. But he wrote them in his own invented language, a series of loops and cursive-looking shapes that occasionally resembled letters. After his death, among stacks of paper, there were some legible notes found. Among them were these messages: "This is true that the great Moses the giver of the tenth commandment appeared in Washington, D.C., April 11, 1931." "This is true that on October 2, 1946, the great Virgin Mary and the Star of Bethlehem appeared over the nation's capital." "This is true that Adam the first man God created appeared in person on January 20, 1949. This was on the day of President Truman's inauguration." "This design

[*The Throne*] is proof of the Virgin Mary descending [*sic*] into Heaven, November 2, 1950. It is also spoken of by Pope Pius XII."

He also wrote a new book of Revelation. Like St. John's Revelation in the New Testament, recorded in a special language on the Isle of Patmos and scribbled onto parchment at the speed of a fever dream, St. James's Revelation was also a kind of stenography from God. On fire with the Spirit when he wrote, he recorded these messages in a spiral notebook. On the cover, in blue U.S. government ink, was scribbled *The Book of the 7 Dispensation by St. James.* Scholars have deemed the book, like the commandments, illegible. The few English words that appear in it, such as "Revelation" and "Virgin Mary," are most often in all caps and misspelled.

6.

"And I saw a new heaven and a new earth: the first heaven and the first earth were passed away . . ." (Revelation 21:1). He knew what that meant, knew the third heaven was the heaven of God, the second heaven was the heaven of the stars and the sun and the moon, and the first heaven, the doomed heaven spoken of in Revelation, was here, now. He was preparing.

He worked through the dark mornings, his joints and back tight as rusty hinges in the damp cold of the garage. Sometimes he'd stop to draw a quick sketch of a plan or to stare at what he was making.

He had built a stage in the back of the garage on which to set some of the pieces. On the larger objects he put rusty metal casters so he could move them to just the right spot. Everything was perfectly symmetrical, had to be, because St. James was remaking time. That's right, *remaking time.* Not just representing time as told in the Bible, he was replicating it with trash. You can see it if you look. On the right is the story of the Old Testament, of Moses and the Law; on the left is the history of Jesus and Grace, the way to salvation.

St. James understood that the time of God, the only time, was cyclical, always returning. No thing, no event, was pointless. Life repeated. It was right there in Ecclesiastes: "The sun also ariseth, and the sun goeth down, and hasteth to his place where he arose . . . The thing that hath been, it is that which shall be; and that which is done is that which shall be done." Death simply meant rebirth and a new, more glorious life in heaven, where you would be reunited with all things lost, with Lee and your father and some of the men from the 385th who had died since the war. If you placed your faith in the Lord Jesus Christ you would never, ever die. Your tears would be wiped away and forgotten. If you placed your faith in Jesus it didn't matter that you cleaned toilets and lived alone, that sometimes the people on your street scared you, called you a crazy fuck, a hermit, that sometimes the voices in your head called you things even worse, things you didn't want to hear; and it didn't matter that so many of the people you loved had vanished from the earth and your life and you could actually feel the empty spaces they left behind. None of it mattered. And if you truly believed, you were not just a poor man alone in the city

among the poor, toiling in a poorly lit garage, babbling to
a brick wall; you were not just a janitor, a forgotten vet
scraping by on a paltry check. Your life mattered now and
forever. Your life actually mattered.

He worked. He covered bottles and jelly jars and light
bulbs with gold and silver foil, which he got from wine bottles
and imported beer bottles and cigarette cartons and boxes of
aluminum wrap. He used the tops of coffee cans for bases.
He mounted upside-down drawers on cheap glass vases,
wrapped them in foil. He trimmed the edges of a sawed-
in-half table with government electrical cable before covering it all in gold foil. He used kraft paper and cardboard
for angels' wings, used carpet rolls to support the greatest
weight. He used glue and nails and pins, and sometimes he
encased an object in layers of foil until it was exactly the
right size and shape.

And then there was *The Throne* itself, the centerpiece
of the huge structure, an old red-plush chair bought sec-
ondhand. He gave it gold wings and put it up high, a seat
for the coming Savior. He gave it a high back—four feet,
five feet?—of wooden shapes and smaller cardboard wings
and bulbs of silver and gold. He named objects for saints
and tacked his walls with biblical quotes and a picture of
Lee, who was now, God told him, an angel living inside
His body, God's body as big as eternity. At the top of it
all, this expanse that filled the entire back of a cold, damp
garage at the end of a dark alley in one of the roughest
neighborhoods in the city of Washington, were the words
"Fear Not."

7.

St. James left the earth before he was ready, before he was finished, even though he once told the merchant he rented the garage from, "*The Throne* is my life. I'll finish it before I die." He had been working on it in the garage for fourteen years, thinking about it perhaps forever, and he wasn't done. He had had stomach cancer for some time, though it had only recently been diagnosed at the free clinic for World War vets. He refused to believe he was dying. It wasn't his time yet. He worked on *The Throne* up to the very end, and the work eased his pain.

Death kept St. James from knowing so many things about his Throne. Like just after his death when the merchant brought a reporter named Ramon Geremia from the *Washington Post* to look at it in the garage, where he poked at it and picked things up and probably didn't quite put them back in the right spot, thus slightly altering *the entire history of time*. And he never got to read the story, which ran under the headline "Tinsel, Mystery Are Sole Legacy of Lonely Man's Strange Vision" on December 15, 1964. And he didn't get to see the filmmaker out there either, the guy with the Beatles haircut, telling everyone in the local art community what an amazing thing *The Throne* was and how a little black janitor with absolutely no friends and an unknown history had made it over many years. He never got to know that critics and scholars would write about his life and work, comparing him to people and movements of which he'd never heard. But most of all, he never got to see *The Throne,* sparkling amidst a field of purple in the Smithsonian

American Museum of Art, never got to stand on those marble floors in his best Sunday suit, his St. James crown glittering on his head, and look at what he'd made using only belief and thrown-away things.

Sentimental, Heartbroken Rednecks

(AN ESSAY ON FAILURE)

Unless a writer is extremely old when he dies, in which case he has probably become a neglected institution, his death must always seem untimely. This is because a real writer is always shifting and changing and searching. The world has many labels for him, of which the most treacherous is the label of Success.

—James Baldwin, "Alas, Poor Richard"

I CAME ACROSS THE STORIES of Breece D'J Pancake, a bent-spined book wedged back among other fictions, while not shelving at a university library when I was twenty. My job, before they "asked me to leave," was late-shift shelver. I chose to work the late shift because no supervisors and very few students were around. My non-shelving went like this: At nine each night I would take a full cart of books—a big, scratched, wooden thing with whistling black wheels the size of golf balls—up to the fourth floor (Quiet Study), find a secluded aisle, and, picking books nearly at random from the

shelves or from the cart I wasn't going to unload, read first
sentences until I found just the right tone and rhythm—sometimes the hard declarative got me, other times a windy, ba-
roque sentence—then sit down and read for a few hours. It
was the most edifying minimum-wage job from which one
could ever hope to get soundly and swiftly canned.

I picked up this particular book—let's say it was a Tuesday
night, air filled with the soft electric drone of a library, a fat
moon hovering in the blue window at the end of the aisle—
because of the unique name down the spine: Breece D'J
Pancake. I had to skip the foreword by Pulitzer Prize–winner
James Alan McPherson, of whom I had never heard, to get to
the real first sentence, in a story called "Trilobites": "I open
the truck's door, step onto the brick side street."

I liked the simplicity, the economy—the speed that comma
generated in the middle of the sentence. I fancied myself
someone who might one day put a pickup truck and a brick
side street in an opening sentence, someone who would write
stories full of brokenhearted loners, based entirely on the
people I knew in Virginia, people who drank Bud and either
worked hard or didn't work at all and never, no matter what,
said what they felt because whatever that might be was surely
killing them; these were people who in fact could not muster
whatever it is inside a human being that allows one to reason through and articulate thoughts and feelings. I was going
to—rather grandly—devote my life to doing it for them.

The characters who crowded my skull back then fum-
bled through meaningless lives toward ambiguously meaningful acts of depravity and violence, acts entirely and only

in *my* control, acts, I hoped, a reader would understand as profoundly significant even if the character went on wallowing in darkness. At twenty I had theories and thoughts in surplus, most of which ended in fantasies of me as famous and thoroughly praised for my deep insight.

In memory—which tends to be fluid and nostalgic, if not downright false—I knew Pancake was a Southerner eleven words in. I felt that largely irrational regional kinship Southerners (or rather writers, critics, and commentators from the South) expend so much energy talking about.

I read on, down through the first paragraph, struck by the honed sentences, the linguistic tension, the somber tone, the imagery: "The air is smoky with summertime. A bunch of starlings swim over me . . . I remember Pop's dead eyes looking at me. They were real dry, and that took something out of me."

I read the twelve stories in the book during my shift (one of my last, it turned out). They were all about outsiders, the working poor of the craggy hills of West Virginia, just a couple of hours from where I live in the Blue Ridge Mountains, a land of satellite dishes on hilltops and the skeletons of rusty pickups slumped uselessly in ivy-filled ravines, a land of leaning trailers and primer-colored cars up on blocks.

Critic and poet Lewis Simpson, in *The Dispossessed Garden* (another book I lucked upon; with enough leisure and curiosity, one can luck one's way right through an entire library wing), wrote: "Southern fiction derive[s] from visions in which faith in the [writer's] ability to make his own world has had an entangled confrontation with an experience of memory and history that tells him he cannot do it." In other words, the writer begins with failure and pushes forward from there—the central metaphor of Original Sin further complicated by family, community, and shared history. This was certainly true of Pancake's stories. They were exhausting exercises in hope and futility, struggle and failure, and, ultimately, in figuring out how to carry on for the next struggle, which was always, though played out in physical terms, moral in nature.

Some of the stories puzzled me. They were open-ended, both bleak and oddly reassuring about the central decency in humans, each offering a kind of raw immediacy and a stunted epiphany. His characters were bighearted dreamers, people trying to do right, yet stymied by economic woes, familial attachment, even the unforgiving landscape of Appalachia. They couldn't win; life presented them with failure and dead dreams as soon as they slithered into the world: from here, they began. I knew what he meant. I felt a little dead back then, reading those stories, cloaked in failure.

It's the old story of Southern art, the one I've been aware of most of my life, I guess, the one you can read in Faulkner, O'Connor, and Welty, the one you can hear in the songs of Hank Williams, Johnny Cash, Lucinda Williams, and Steve Earle: *We're utterly defeated, doomed to live out our genealogical and historical unhappiness, but not without a bloody sort of passion and genuine tears.* We celebrate the noble fuckup, the hero as lost cause. And like the above-named artists, Pancake's greatest strength as a writer was to render in words a moment, toward the end of each story—stories

oddly akin to good country songs, to old ballads—of uncomfortably authentic pain and confession, a moment when
reader and writer unite within character, creating—ever so
briefly—a perfect, universal instant of empathy.

The stories were tragic to the extreme, biblical in power,
yet they possessed a rare honesty and vulnerability. The style
was Sherwood Anderson or Ernest Hemingway—spare yet
poetic, hard and direct.

I took the book home that night to read the foreword
and afterword, to find out about Breece Pancake.

By the time I was reading the foreword and afterword that
evening when I was twenty, Pancake had been dead for
twelve years. Four years before the posthumous publication
of *The Stories of Breece D'J Pancake,* on Palm Sunday, 1979,
he sat in a lawn chair behind his apartment in Charlottesville,
Virginia, where he had attended graduate school, and placed
the butt of an over-and-under .20 gauge shotgun on the soft
wet ground in front him. He leaned forward, letting the steel
barrel click against his teeth, and pulled the trigger. He was
twenty-six.

Four years later, had he been alive, he would have realized the major success he had always dreamed of, the fame
and thorough praise for his insight, standing at the forefront
of a virtual renaissance in Appalachian fiction that included
such writers as Bobbie Ann Mason, Jayne Anne Phillips,
Cormac McCarthy, and Denise Giardina.

I've thought of Pancake a lot since then. I've read his best stories—"Trilobites," "Hollow," "In the Dry," "The Honored Dead"—over and over with admiration, always stunned by their precision and sincerity. The people he wrote about, his people, as the idiom goes, are much like my people. I see some of what I think of as my place in his place. And, sometimes frighteningly, I see myself, the writer, in a shared context with him, the writer.

I understand that the better one gets at writing, the more one can do with language, form it and reform it like so much clay, pack it with density or strip it down, the harder writing gets, the more your own sentences can sound like bullshit and lies in your head, the more your failures—which frankly almost no one but you even cares about—can weigh you down psychically and depress you.

I graduated from the creative writing program at the University of Virginia two decades after Pancake did, held the same fellowship, walked through the same halls, studied with some of the same professors. And though there is always a macabre pull to focus on the tragic, grisly, and sad—I feel it right now—it is Pancake's small body of work and his life that have always interested me: how his life not only informed his writing, but was his writing.

He thought of himself as a work in progress, and he was hard on his work, hard on himself as a worker. His mother, Helen Pancake, in a letter to James Alan McPherson concerning the publication of *The Stories* in 1983 by Little, Brown, wrote, "Jim, 'bullshit' was one of B's choice sayings—in fact he used to say he wanted his short stories entitled 'Bullshit Artist.' Love his heart!"

Here was a young writer who would often write fifteen to twenty drafts of a story (long before word processors, when you had to literally rewrite a story), struggled every day with the craft of writing, every second, it seems, pondering the large moral questions he addressed in his work. Considering the importance he placed on his fiction, a remark like "bullshit artist," even if said with an aw-shucks grin, shows just how self-deprecating he could be. When your work is your life, losing faith in it means you can't look in the mirror.

Many people, including National Book Award–winning novelist John Casey, who still teaches one semester a year at the University of Virginia, have called Pancake an "aristocrat in blue jeans," a young man "wise beyond his years," concerned with an older set of values and traditions from Appalachia, those handed over from Europe and early Christianity and then cordoned off by geographic isolation and small and all but static populations. Statements like these, coupled with his still fragmented biography, have surrounded the life and work of Pancake with an almost James Dean–like mythology among writers and Southern and Appalachian literary scholars.

By all accounts, though, he did view himself as chivalrous, striving for a kind of Old World nobility in a time when notions of nobility had more to do with material acquisition and upbringing than character or deeds. He thought of life

as something to face with your fists clenched and then con-
quer, and he would come to think of his fictions as a kind of
mission—the most important thing he had—to mine the
depths of himself and the world to get at what was real and
pure and vital. To dispense, in fact, with bullshit.

Pancake was born in Milton, West Virginia, in 1952 as
Breece Dexter Pancake. He attended West Virginia Wesleyan
in Buckhannon for two years, then graduated from Marshall
University in 1974. He spent time traveling out West, working
odd jobs, then took a position teaching English at Fork Union
Military Academy (where, twenty-three years later, I would
be offered—and would decline—the same job), forty miles
southeast of Charlottesville. In January of 1975, he began
attending John Casey's writing workshop at the University of
Virginia. Casey saw him as prodigiously talented, and he and
Pancake would later become close friends.

Many things happened in 1975 that greatly changed
Pancake's life. His father, C. R. Pancake, died of complications from multiple sclerosis on September 8 in Milton. Less
than three weeks later, on September 29, Pancake's longtime
best friend and drinking buddy, Matthew Heard, was killed
in a car accident in West Virginia. In October, still reeling
and angry and sad and vulnerable, he met award-winning
Southern novelists Mary Lee Settle and Peter Taylor, relationships he would keep and foster until his death four
years later.

In one year, Pancake must have felt that he had lost everything and at the same time gained a new life. Most of the baggage and connections to home were gone, vanished in an instant. And suddenly some of the best writers in the country at ostensibly one of the best writing programs in the country viewed him as the real thing, an artist, seemed, in fact, to admire his work in a way they might a peer's as opposed to a student's.

Months later he was officially accepted to both the Iowa Writers' Workshop and the writing program at the University of Virginia, choosing the latter. He was on his way, wishing his father and Matthew were around to see it.

In the foreword to *The Stories*, McPherson describes Pancake as "constitutionally . . . a lonely and melancholy man." Certainly now, after the loss of his father and best friend, he was even more so.

In Charlottesville, where he finally moved in 1976, he lived in a dingy one-room apartment at 1 Blue Ridge Lane (where there is now a neighborhood of half-million-dollar homes and a nearby country club). His desk, where he kept the many drafts of his stories, was a piece of plywood set up on sawhorses in a corner.

He kept to himself, as always, gregarious on a superficial level but never letting anyone get too close to him. If he thought he was making someone uncomfortable with his loud voice or Southern drawl, he would apologize politely and vanish, go off by himself and not be heard from for days.

In Charlottesville, which is in one of the wealthiest counties in the United States, and at the University of Virginia, which is notoriously conservative (in the relative world of universities) and filled, it seems, with the upwardly mobile children of America's most privileged, Pancake stuck out like, well, a six-foot-plus, bearded West Virginian with an accent that connoted the lower classes, wearing old blue jeans, a leather jacket, and a pair of shit-kicker cowboy boots; this among a student population with an inordinate number of young people who have attended operas, polo matches, and debutante balls throughout their lives.

I remember days of chilly vibes myself in those hallowed halls, and this was two decades later and, presumably, in a university with a now far more tolerant and diversified environment. I once attended a lecture by a stuffy and moderately famous poet in which he talked about the ingenious use of space in the trailers of the rural poor (for instance, you could put your child's Big Wheel on the kitchen counter when it was raining; this had somehow been turned into a poststructuralist book of some sort containing photographs and an abstruse, utterly condescending essay), and it was all I could do not to hurl a stack of books at him. Pancake, to say the least, did not fit in at Mr. Jefferson's university. When he wasn't writing, or hunting or fishing or hiking in the Blue Ridge Mountains along the same Appalachian trails that begin just a few miles from my home, he spent most of his social time among other writers, McPherson and Casey particularly, who were also his teachers.

All writers, at least all the ones I know, regardless of background, gender, or ethnicity, tend to be outsiders to some degree, socially guarded, a little scorched on the inside, entranced by the world yet not quite trusting it completely, so he felt most comfortable among them and appreciated what they had to offer him—their experience, the names of authors that inspired them, a good stiff drink (interestingly, one of Pancake's favorite writers was Jack London, author of the blackly hilarious *Martin Eden,* which is about a writer who becomes successful and finds he much preferred his far more understandable and less maddening failure).

Also in 1976, he began going to the maximum-security prison in Jarrett (where I have relatives) to talk to and teach prisoners, eventually helping a young inmate publish some of his poetry. He considered this a duty, not charity, an Old World act of *noblesse oblige.* For the most part, however, Pancake stayed true to his "lonely and melancholy" nature, leaning over his plywood desk at 1 Blue Ridge Lane, arranging and rearranging words and sentences until he felt they contained little pieces of him. Then he would put a line through them and begin again. They were all wrong.

In June of 1977, Pancake, who had been raised in what I'd call mild Protestantism—as opposed, say, to Southern Baptism or Pentecostalism or other evangelical denominations common to his (and my) region of birth—converted to Catholicism, and he officially became a novitiate in the Church just before his twenty-fifth birthday.

He found in Catholicism the kind of rigid moral code he sought, one that did not bend to fit the shape of the cultural moment. He valued ideas and things from an older time, a time he'd only read about, and had little patience for ideological fads and trends. Though he was not, according to those closest to him, judgmental toward the behavior of others, it seems safe to say he became a staunch conservative. The strictness of the Catholic Church—the clearly defined values—coincided with what he expected from himself, what he explored in his stories. He took the Catholic name John (writer of the Book of Revelation), making himself Breece Dexter John Pancake.

A month earlier, in May, *The Atlantic* had accepted "Trilobites" for publication in their December issue. It was his first acceptance in a major magazine. But he didn't gloat, didn't become smug with success; rather, he doubted his ability to live up to his own high standards even more. He felt, in low moments, that he was a fraud, a true Martin Eden, and now he'd convinced an editor at a big, important magazine that he was somehow a real writer. Here is what he'd wanted—what he'd struggled for at that plywood desk with the pictures of his father and Matthew on it—and now he was sad and ridiculous because he suddenly knew that the people out there deeming literary work worthy or unworthy were utterly lacking in taste, possibly as fraudulent as he was. I think of Walker Percy's famous opening passage in *The Second Coming:* "In fact, he didn't even realize he was depressed. Rather was it the world and life around him which seemed to grow more senseless and farcical with each passing day."

When he received the check for the story, he wired his mother flowers and took James McPherson to dinner, where he drank like a man drowning his sorrows. McPherson described him on this night as far from pleased with himself, instead "morose and nervous." He felt like he'd just been given the keys to the world, only to find out that the world wasn't much.

He began working even harder—at writing, at life; maybe that was the answer. Daniel Menaker at *The New Yorker* solicited a story in November of 1977. Pancake worked through mornings, drank alone through most nights, never missed mass on Sundays, prayed and doubted himself. In February, *The Atlantic* accepted "In the Dry." In March, *Nightwork* accepted "Time and Again." At twenty-five he was quickly becoming the center of a literary buzz.

Around this time, he asked John Casey to be his godfather in the Church. In the afterword of *The Stories,* Casey writes: "This godfather arrangement soon turned upside down. Breece started getting after me about going to mass, going to confession, instructing my daughters. It wasn't so much out of righteousness as out of gratitude and affection, but he could be blistering . . . As with his other knowledge and art, he took in his faith with intensity, almost as if he had a different, deeper measure of time. He was soon an older Catholic than I was."

❖

In March of 1978, Wendy Jacobson, on the basis of a couple of Pancake's stories, solicited a novel for Doubleday. He began making notes, writing character sketches, telling friends about his good fortune, acting, in fact, like someone who expected to live a long time.

In 1983, *The Stories* was nominated for the Pulitzer Prize for fiction and the Weatherford Prize for the best book about Appalachia. Joyce Carol Oates, in the *New York Times,* compared the debut to Hemingway's *In Our Time.* The critical acclaim was overwhelming and unanimous. *The Stories of Breece D'J Pancake* has never gone out of print. If I try, I mean if I really try, I can almost consider that a happy ending.

Henry Miller once said that literature was the common life, examined and exalted. E. M. Cioran intimated that only literature about the pauper or the bum, the life all but lost, is interesting, because the powerful in society are not even real but rather figments or projections, elaborate constructs, with important-sounding titles (I think what Cioran, that poet of nihilism, meant is that deep down we are all paupers, some of us just insist on perpetuating the elaborate charade that we are not).

Sometimes I think they're talking about Pancake. He struggled on the page and in life. He examined and exalted in story after story, holding created lives still for a few tightly focused pages, distilling moments of chaos into instants of crystalline meaning and morose poetry.

But life is murkier—you can't contain it in the biggest book, can you?—hard on those who can't find temperance. Life is without rhetorical shape, regardless of how rigid your chosen system of values.

Pancake was a moralist, a humanist, in the strictest Christian sense. His characters begin, wearing Original Sin like their own flesh, caught up in a world where they seem destined to struggle and fail and pay for their failure—gospel music or bluegrass chiseled into diamond-hard prose.

Pancake's favorite biblical verses were Revelation 3:15–16: "I know thy works, that thou art neither cold nor hot: I would thou wert cold or hot. So then because thou art lukewarm, and neither cold nor hot, I will spue thee out of my mouth." Fitting verses for a writer, a man, who seems to have been nothing but cold or hot, yet always, dangerously, perceiving himself as lukewarm, somehow failing, failing, failing, savoring the acceptances and adulation for only a second and dwelling endlessly on—replaying in his head—every rejection and humiliating disappointment that any life of art, even the most successful one, is necessarily full of.

Pancake was hard on his characters, yes—a bit like pulling the wings off an insect and watching it bang its head against the inside of a jar—but he also always let them see, if only for a second, a glimpse of light in all that darkness. In the last line of perhaps his best-known story, "Trilobites," he sets a boy named Colley free of all that came before with a deceptively simple declarative statement: "I feel my fear moving away in rings through time for a million years."

He was not, however, so kind to himself.

❖

In early 1979, he began giving all of his possessions away; "gifts," he said, because he would be leaving Charlottesville soon. He had applied for a couple of writing fellowships with residencies, had some teaching opportunities, was working hard on the novel. Because he never let anyone get too close—not even Casey or McPherson—and given his extraordinary success at such a young age, friends thought he was fine; just Breece being Breece: difficult as hell, always up for a good argument, hard-drinking and a little sad, but genuinely kind, decent, and generous.

He wrote an encouraging letter to a friend and fellow writer. On the envelope, Pancake had changed the return address from "1 Blue Ridge Lane" to "One Blow Out Your Brain." To another friend he wrote, "If I weren't a good Catholic, I'd consider getting a divorce from life." Yet it was only in hindsight that these messages were perceived as portentous (Pancake was famous for his black humor).

On Palm Sunday 1979, he used the only shotgun he hadn't given away to kill himself. I have no idea, nor does anyone, how intentional or accidental his suicide was, how deep-seated or fleeting his darkest thoughts. Maybe he'd been planning it since his father and Matthew died, or since that first story was accepted and he saw the beginnings of the absurd shape of success. Maybe, as Cheever once wrote, Pancake was "deeply conscious of chaos, as if we were in the act of falling from some atmospheric and moral orbit, as if the sweet seriousness of life were in great danger."

III.

The Metaphor

Ellis, a twenty-seven-year-old black neighbor the young writer never met or spoke to, was shot in the stomach by a rookie police officer and killed. The writer was twenty-three, unemployed. His neighborhood in Richmond, Virginia, was low-rent, mixed race, volatile, the only place he could afford. He had bars on his windows. He had $56.74, according to his journal. He had a mattress, some clothes, some books, some CDs. He did not, now, have much else. Except for time on his hands, curiosity.

FACT 1
When Ellis was shot he had been fleeing the scene of what resembled a robbery. The shooting was the reason the two guys in front of the writer's apartment—Ellis's former friends and roommates at the same halfway—were torturing the old, abandoned couch.

EVIDENCE 1

The couch: The couch slumped three-legged on the cracked, weed-sprouting sidewalk—yellow, filthy, full of holes and protruding springs like rusty antennae. Drunks and runaways often slept on it; prostitutes, male and female and males dressed as females, rested on it, and sometimes there were shouting arguments or fistfights on or near it. It was not a pleasant thing to have sitting in front of your apartment, the writer thought. At the same time, he was fascinated by almost everything that happened here.

FACT 2

It was ten or eleven o'clock when the commotion around the couch started.

The writer—who, it should be pointed out, was not *really* a writer, except in his mind (by which I mean he had not written any books)—looked out his window, through the bars, keeping his lights off so the two guys couldn't see him. They were yelling, cursing. They were familiar to the writer, but he didn't know them. The halfway they lived in was directly next door to his apartment in a line of row houses that had been built during Civil War reconstruction.

He, the writer, made a point at this time, just months after he'd moved in, just months after he had had some problems I won't bother to mention, not to talk to any of his neighbors, especially the ones from the halfway, because it was as if, he thought, their whole sad lives were contained on their faces, in their blank, sometimes angry stares as they sat on the porch bumming one another's cigarettes and whistling sarcastically at the transvestite whores.

And the writer wanted to believe, wanted to *nurture the delusion,* that he had nothing in common with these people beyond a conspicuous lack of money. When you're down, I mean *down*—when the world looks like every little promise has been lanced and bled out—you need a story to tell yourself. The young writer told himself the one about how he didn't belong here.

ASSAILANTS

One of the two assailants of the couch was a gigantic black guy—probably three hundred pounds—with an Afro that he would sometimes part in the middle, sending it out in two directions. He always wore the same hooded black sweatshirt and baggy jeans that covered most of his bright white basketball sneakers.

The other guy was thin and of Asian extraction. He wore a leather jacket with the name of a band on the back. Ether or Kepone or Nitrous, something that was just one word, chemical, punk. I can't remember. I mean, *he* can't remember.

FACT 3

A bottle broke, sending shards of glittering glass across the sidewalk and street, some of it hitting the van that had been parked along the curb, inert, for months. I mention this here because it was the sort of image the writer expended a great deal of energy attempting to poeticize. Glass like quartz, like diamonds, like teeth, etc. Yeah, he was *that* kind of writer.

FACT 4

The writer didn't know about his neighbor Ellis yet, who had been dead now for several hours, not even his name, or about how he'd been shot in the stomach, dropped shivering into a puddle of his own warm blood.

GATHERING INFO

The next day, however, the day after the night of the couch torturing, even though he was so frightened he could taste bile in the back of his mouth, the writer walked up to the giant black guy as he sat on the steps of the halfway, smoking a cigarette.

The writer smiled uncomfortably, falsely, looking at the black guy's Afro. He had a big blue comb, the kind with a rounded handle which were popular in the seventies, perched atop his head, half buried in hair. The writer wondered what brought him here—schizophrenia, drugs, a minor chemical imbalance, or had he just been released from jail. He seemed perfectly sane.

Writer wondered. Writer stared.

You got a eye problem?

The writer said yes, he usually wore glasses, which was the truth but came out all wrong, and for a second he waited for the black guy to get up and try to split his face open with his huge black fists. But the black guy smiled; he had a sense of humor. The writer instantly felt better.

He asked him about the couch, said that he was just wondering.

Why the fuck you wondering? the black guy said, but it didn't sound threatening; more like: Why would anyone care?

He said he was just curious, that maybe one day, when he didn't live around here anymore, he'd want to write about it.

Smiling, the black guy offered the writer a cigarette. He turned out to be a nice guy. A writer, he said, laughing. Bet there's a lot of writers around here.

The writer told him he once published a story in an "avant-garde" journal he was sure nobody ever read, the kind of thing that surprises you with its existence. He told him they paid him thirty dollars. The black guy laughed.

They kept talking.

When the writer mentioned the couch again, which was just a black stain on the sidewalk now, the black guy told him his version of Ellis. Later the writer looked in the paper. Sure enough, there was the Ellis story—two paragraphs in the back of the Metro section. The two versions of the story were entirely different, though, as you might imagine. Later the writer would think that you had to let speculation in to understand this at all.

ANTHONY'S STORY (SUMMARIZED)

According to Anthony (that was the black guy's name, Anthony, so from now on I will stop referring to him as "the black guy," which I don't *think* is offensive, but then again, who knows), Ellis was smoking crack. Smoking it all the time. The person who ran the halfway, a city social worker, found a glass pipe and kicked him out. They had a very strict policy about drugs.

Ellis, suddenly homeless, went to his ex-wife's apartment down in the tenements (they weren't ex officially—and Anthony took a long time to explain this part—because it cost about a thousand dollars to get a divorce in Virginia and they didn't have that kind of money; so they were still married but they pretended to be divorced).

Ellis had two kids. Two boys, fairly young. His not-really-ex-wife was pregnant again, but this one wasn't his, which hurt, in a way, but was also a relief. He couldn't afford the first two, much less the third.

Ellis stood in the doorway of his not-really-ex-wife's apartment, smiling, or trying to, but looking more like he was gritting his teeth to stave off some unbearable pain. His lips were blue, or purple. His eyes were yellow, red veins squiggling in every direction like secondary roads on an old map. He had no saliva. His mouth, extending down his throat to his roiling guts, was lined with fur and dust and cobwebs. He was jonesing bad, said Anthony. He acted *aggressively,* said the paper.

Ellis asked his not-really-ex-wife for money: ten bucks, five bucks, a buck. She said something to the effect of Fuck you. He hit her. Hard. He had to, really. She obviously wanted him to die. Because that's what he was doing, right now, in this dimly lit, roach- and rat-infested hallway, dying. He had often beaten his wife during the marriage (or while they lived together and were married). Ellis loved her so much it made him crazy, Anthony said, made him get high and want to kill her so other people couldn't touch her, couldn't learn her thoughts, so she couldn't go around snuffing out the last cooling embers of his heart with those high heels.

But Anthony assured the writer that she could take it and get up swinging. She often, he said, kicked Ellis's ass. Once she stabbed him in the hipbone with a steak knife. They used to be in love, Anthony said, really seriously in love, and sometimes, you know, that makes people want to do terrible, terrible things.

Ellis knocked her down this time. Then he went into his son's room—the older one's, if the writer heard the story right—to take stuff, money or just things he might be able to sell, quickly, to somebody on the street. Only his son, who was twelve, said Fuck you, too, you ain't my dad, and the truth is, again according to Anthony, nobody really knew if he was actually the father or not.

Ellis "freaked." Nobody respected him anymore. He'd changed this kid's diapers, sat up all night with him once when he was sick. Eyes closed, swinging wildly, he cracked open his son's—or probably his son's—face like a rotten cantaloupe. He started breaking stuff around the apartment—a radio, a picture frame, a mirror.

Then he broke the Nintendo Game Boy he had bought for his son two Christmases ago, back when he was working nights at the condom factory on the south side of Richmond, near the cigarette factories, back before the crack and the couple of short stints in county and the halfway and more crack and then the getting kicked out of the halfway and the needing crack and this sad scene in the government-housing tenements.

Ellis started crying. Bawling. He didn't want to live like this. He hated violence, really—it made him physically sick sometimes—but what else did he have, especially now, feeling like he did?

He stopped, stood still. The room, the building, the city, the spinning earth, hummed softly under his feet. His cranium was lined with wet moss. There was an itch at the center of his being that could only be scratched by a nice lungful of crack smoke (Anthony knew a lot about the specifics of crack, but the writer didn't ask how).

There was a lot of screaming in the apartment, but Ellis didn't hear it because he was standing in his own closed-off, soundproof capsule of regret, holding a smashed Nintendo Game Boy.

Ellis got it in his mind, which was not in a good state right now, to get his son—or most likely his son—who was bleeding badly, whom he was sorry for hitting, whom he loved, deep down, a Nintendo Game Boy. Tonight. A new one. He didn't have any money, of course. He'd spent it all on crack. That's why he was here, why all this commotion had just taken place, why his eyeballs were filled with sand, why his numb teeth wiggled like loose nails fastened up into his bony face, a big part of why he was crying. The circularity, the mind-bending cruelty of the whole episode, made his jaw tighten, the veins in his neck pulse.

Ellis decided to change the direction of his life, right now, by getting a Game Boy. Oh, you've heard that before—druggy decides to change his life while scraping his gaunt face against the bottom of his existence—but this is a story, or at least notes for a story, remember, even if it's true, or at the very least based on a verifiable truth, so let's give Ellis the benefit of the doubt for the next few pages. (I don't know if you believe in God, or anything God-like, but the young writer did, in his own way, or wanted to, in his own way—I mean, he was reading Buber and Tillich and Merton—so he tried to imagine that God's light, God's beautiful beautiful light, shined, or at least *could shine*, in all of us, including himself, Ellis, and Anthony.) And let's do Anthony that favor in particular, because in truth this is mostly Anthony's story and the writer has just tried to get it all down here with a minimum of editorial intrusion.

ANTHONY'S THEORY OF TRAGEDY

Ellis was now paranoid and superstitious and that broken Game Boy became like a voodoo doll in his hand, a palm-sized, cracked symbol of what he'd become. He had to get a new one. He picked up some of the broken stuff, set it on an old folding card table. His oldest son was on the bed, a blood soaked pillow over his face. His wife was wailing and promising to kill him: *I'm going to kill your motherfucking ass, motherfucker!* All the neighbors in the tenement had locked their green-painted metal doors, turned up the sound on their rent-to-own TVs.

Ellis took off, left the tenements, walked and cried and thought it over. People in the writer's neighborhood (he was reading Georges Bernanos's *The Diary of a Country Priest*, which he had just found in a used bookstore, as Ellis walked under his window, so he never saw him) were actually crossing the street to avoid him, which hurt his feelings. They could sense the broken Game Boy in the front pocket of his army coat, he thought.

He started making a lot of noise now, sniffling, groaning, half-talking to the low hum in the concrete he felt in the bottoms of his old, stolen shoes. A new Nintendo Game Boy was his last chance.

Ellis decided to peacefully rob—very low-key, in and out—the 7-Eleven a block from the writer's apartment and the halfway and the couch, a place the writer walked to every morning to buy coffee and a copy of the *Post* and pick up a free copy of a slim paper produced by ex-cons and current inmates, which he found fascinating, and usually to give one homeless person or another his change because it was easier than smiling and saying no, even though, technically, he needed his change (how was he going to get a paper and coffee?).

Ellis walked into the store, browsed. He knocked over a basket of muffins by the coffee machines. He looked like a zombie in a bad late-night movie—eyes bugging out of his head, skin ashy, the corners of his lips white, pasty. The three clerks' eyes followed him, heads swinging around slowly like surveillance cameras.

THE "ATTACK"

Ellis picked up one of those plastic knives they have by the Slurpee machine, for microwave burritos, spreading mustard on your hot dog. He waved it around threateningly.

Empty the register, he said, but his throat was raw from smoking crack. It came out low, like a soft growl.

What? said one clerk.

He repeated himself, which angered him, because he wanted to be the kind of person who only said things once. There were a few customers in the 7-Eleven. They didn't even stop what they were doing.

Get out of here, the young clerk said.

There was, obviously, a metaphysical tinge to the moment (this is how the writer would later think about this material): Ellis was fighting to save his own soul, to save his relationship with his son, or the kid who was most likely his son, to save whatever chance he still had at life. He imagined wrapping up the Game Boy in nice paper with a bow, presenting it to his son. He needed just a few tens out of the drawer. And the clerk, this guy with a goatee and nose ring, wearing a green frock, a guy who played bass badly in a local punk band, was being condescending.

Ellis took a swipe at him, gave him a small scrape on the top of his hand, the one that went, clumsily, on the neck of the bass. The clerk looked at his hand. There was a red abrasion, but no blood. He looked at Ellis and shook his head in annoyance. Then he called the cops. He put his hand over the mouthpiece of the phone and said, leering at Ellis, This is the cops. *On the phone.*

EVIDENCE 2

A chocolate-covered cherry, baseball cards: Ellis grabbed a chocolate-covered cherry, a few packs of baseball cards, and ran out.

THE "SHOWDOWN"

The cops pulled up alongside him before he'd made it very far (the neighborhood was, for obvious reasons, heavily patrolled). They told him, through a speaker, to stop running. Anthony thought that the clerk said Ellis had a knife without specifying that it was plastic, would barely cut through a hot burrito.

Ellis wouldn't stop. He couldn't. He was on a mission. He just kept running, thinking about how he was going to buy his son a Game Boy, give him a big hug, maybe hang around, play him a game of computer football. He would do that for his son. He was going to change.

Finally, he stopped, put his hands up, and turned around. They had a spotlight on him. Trash fled up the street. Ellis couldn't see anything but white light in the direction of the cop car. It was high-volt halogen and angelic. He would just explain himself, he thought. He started walking toward the light.

He reached into the front pocket of his army jacket to pull out the broken Game Boy, evidence to the truth of his story, the importance of his mission, the essential, though perhaps damaged, goodness he knew he still had in his heart.

His throat was scorched, so as he walked quickly toward them to show them the evidence, he was mumbling, saying a lot of things that the cops couldn't understand, panicky crackhead stuff, excuses that sounded great in his mind but somehow morphed into nonsense while laid over in his dry mouth.

They told him to stop and take his hand out of his coat.

A white rookie cop, using a standard-issue .38 caliber pistol, shot him in the stomach as he started walking more quickly toward them with his hand still in his coat.

DEATH SCENE

Ellis's coat opened and out dropped the baseball cards, the plastic knife, the chocolate-covered cherry, and the broken Nintendo Game Boy. The bullet made a clean path through his flesh and muscle and organs and ruptured the aorta, adjacent to his spine. His body cavity filled with blood, putting pressure on his lungs, impeding his breathing. He bled a polluted river of memories and regrets from his mouth. Technically speaking, he was about to suffocate.

His eyes stayed open, wobbled momentarily, as if he was staring up into the descending asses of angels. Because angels, the writer would later think, are projections from the world, from human consciousness and imagination, they would, at this late date, as they fell from the sky for Ellis, be equipped with enormous cunts and cocks, with assholes and o-shaped mouths, would look, in fact, like AMAZINGLY LIFE-LIKE!® sex dolls with dirty wings.

Ellis died right there on the cold sidewalk, in a spreading puddle of his own warm blood, which, if anyone would have checked, had a very high content of cocaine and alcohol.

ANTHONY CONCLUDES

You're lucky to be white, Anthony said to the young writer at the end of his version of the story. If Ellis was white, he'd be alive. I bet they would have just used a taser on you, or mace.

He was right, of course—the writer knew that if he had done the same thing he would not have been shot. Beaten and arrested, certainly, but not dead. And if, let's say, they did shoot him, he'd have gotten a page or so somewhere near the front of the paper. He'd have gotten a narrative: tragic death of troubled suburban blah blah blah. People like Ellis, as you know, don't get the *privilege* of a narrative.

That was the end of Anthony's story, or rather the part of this story for which his information is mostly responsible.

WE NEED AN ENDING

But we need to continue. The writer could not take this story as it was—the hard, ridiculous facts, the two empty, antiseptic paragraphs tucked into the back of the paper. He *could not take it.*

So, in an effort to save this story from its hopelessness and violence and stupidity, in an effort to resuscitate some *modicum* of meaning, he turned to the couch.

The writer was intrigued even more now by the couch as an image carrying weight, as a metaphor for something, anything: rage, sorrow, something. Once he realized that the couch and Ellis were a part of the same story, that there were unseen connections all over this section of this Southern city, he felt as if he'd solved some utterly pointless puzzle with nothing to do but take it apart and start over again.

That was the thing about the writer—he was always mulling things over, often rather depressingly, looking for, or trying to invent, just the smallest glimmer of sense. This was selfish, he knew, because *he* was the one who needed saving.

So here comes the real ending, which is, if not happy, at least active and not passive and pointless and bloody: the night of Ellis's death, the writer was looking out his window, as I said, at the two guys, Anthony and the skinny Asian punk rocker, beating up the couch that lived in front of his apartment.

They hit it with a baseball bat. They threw bottles at it. When they sprayed it with lighter fluid and lit it on fire, the writer thought he'd better call the cops. Then he decided against it. He was new here, and he didn't want to be known as someone who called the cops.

He figured the couch was surrounded by concrete. What could happen? He watched them burn and curse the couch, as if it were evil, as if it was somehow a whole squadron of the one cop who shot Ellis, as if it had taken everything that had ever meant anything to them and destroyed it without a thought.

It was quite a blaze! Their shadows went dancing crazy up apartment building walls. And the fire department didn't show up for half an hour. In fact, the couch, that hive of disease, that beacon for fighting and illegal communing in front of the writer's apartment, was black springs and charred foam by the time they arrived—smoking cinders, a rectangular black stain, a ruined metaphor in need of a story.

Secret History of Home Cinema

A CHILD APPEARS ON SCREEN, grainy and out of focus, shimmering in dull pastels. It is the simplest of home movies: a child outside, in a blue plastic pool, knee-deep in water. You watch the picture get bumped onto the wall and then back onto the old vinyl screen as some cousin or brother or sister adjusts the focus, aligns the images.

You are here, in this dark and crowded living room, with your friend (soon to be your lover, but that comes later). The boy in the film is connected to your friend, whose hand you are holding—the child of your friend's divorced sister who has had her problems but is now, you heard after dinner, *straightening up, getting back on track,* et cetera. Your friend knows the history of this child, his idiosyncrasies, the fact that he wets himself still, that he speaks only in fragmentary English, that his mother's boyfriend, Robert, who set up the film and gathered the family around, drinks too much, *leads an unexamined life,* and is probably the *product of abuse,* according to your friend.

You know—because of the buzz of extended-family gossip—that this child was caught in kindergarten stuffing his own feces up the bathroom spigot to make the water brown, an action that seemed, at the moment you heard about it, replete with so many dark possibilities that it was, literally, beyond reply. So you nodded, with a straight face.

Your friend warned you about the family on the way here in the car, providing a brief summary of almost everyone in the room with you now. But that kind of briefing, the let-me-warn-you-about my-family kind, is always either downplayed or exaggerated, placing the truth somewhere in between extremes.

You sip your drink as Robert appears onscreen with the child, and you wonder who's holding the camera. The mother? The child, the real child as opposed to his image onscreen, is sleeping in the grandmother's bedroom with his mother, who had a headache. Robert, the flesh-and-blood Robert, is telling you how 16 mm film is superior to video, how it still has the possibilities of art contained in its makeup, although not much commercial viability. He says how he was going to go to film school until he *realized you have to eat, ha ha.* And you thank God for capitalism.

[cut to: thumb, grass, water . . .]

The child bounces in the pool, orange floats with duck heads surrounding his biceps, his small stomach distended in the way of young children not yet programmed to suck in their guts, like everyone in the room is doing after the large meal.

The cousin or brother or sister turns up the sound. You haven't connected names to faces yet, and you're a little drunk and it's too dark to see anyway. The audio sputters in sync with the shifting images. Lines resembling insects appear and vanish.

The camera is a remarkable thing, you think, with its ability to transform the mundane into an immortal moment able to travel through time, reappear days or months or years after its actual occurrence. Every second of our existence is alive with possibility, but we don't see it until we hit rewind, until we freeze the frame. It is sad that so many things, all suffused with meaning, escape the unaided eye.

[cut to: darkness, bare feet, a baseball field, the child in a hat too big for his head . . .]

Okay, hit the ball. Give it a good one, says Robert from out of camera range, his voice slightly higher through the filter of the machine.

The angles are crude, amateurish—wide pans, pointless close-ups, the field tilting like an airplane wing. There is no craft at work here, no politic or sociology, no aesthetics: it's random, accidental, honest.

It hurts, says the child. Don't want to. He is looking at the ground, hugging himself with one arm as he chews, actually *chews,* on his other hand. The bat is at his feet.

Pick up the bat and hit the ball, says Robert. The film's rolling. Do you want the whole world to see you acting like a retard? Just think, millions of people out there in TV land seeing how much of a baby you are, how you won't even try to hit a baseball.

You turn your head, glancing at your friend, the person who brought you here, deeper inside these strangers' lives than you want to be. Your friend is drinking an imported beer, leaning back, seemingly bored by the flickering images. *[cut to: trees, sky, ground, feet . . .]*

The boy is holding the bat now, pathetically, you think, letting it hang over the back of his shoulder.

All right all right all right, boy, knock this thing into outer space, to the next planet. Ready?

It hurts, says the boy. The child chews his hand again, looking away from the voice and the camera, as if he were averting his eyes from you. The bat slips from his hand and hits the ground. He begins crying, silently, or at least not loud enough to be captured on audio.

Pick up the bat, retard, says Robert. Your mom's going to see this. She'll know that you can't even have fun without crying.

Your friend is calm beside you, slowly sipping the beer. The same person who fascinated you by being so aware only hours ago. The person who talks endlessly about progressive politics, who rambles on about French deconstruction and friends' dissertations and David Cronenberg's sexualizing of technological gadgetry and the pre-postmodern self-effacing irony of Chaplin and Shepard's dialogue in *Paris, Texas,* and how that film was *really about human suffering, you know;* the person who talks about writing a book about you can't remember what, but it seemed deep at the time you first heard it, at the end of your first date/get-to-know-each-other/casual thing, as the two of you smoked a joint and later had your first kiss and thought of making love but didn't because you wanted it to be special, meaning semi-sober, and later, after a nice dinner and conversation and maybe discussion of the greater philosophical questions concerning love and the soul and whether people actually had *soul mates,* which made you laugh a little, even though secretly you were hopeful, wanting more than anything an easy human connection, love, or something like love, without all the fucking work. This same friend, this soon-to-be lover, is motionless and stone-faced as the child cries on the screen.

Robert, leaning toward you in confidence and, you assume, a gesture of camaraderie, says how the kid is a basket case, how his father, whom Robert calls an asshole, just took off and left the kid and his mother. Just like that. He tells you how the kid needs discipline and hard lessons, how the kid will adjust to a strict, yet loving, environment and be a better person for it. He tells you how he had to do something because the mother, your friend's sister, whom you met earlier at dinner while both of you hit the wine a little too hard, just couldn't handle him anymore with the copro . . . copra . . . corpa . . . playing-with-shit stuff.

You feel his breath in your ear as the child chews his hand on the screen.

[cut to: child, smiling, at home plate, holding the bat over his shoulder . . .]

Okay, buddy, that was good. Good hit. But hold on to the bat like I showed you, says Robert, who must have been holding the camera to his eye as he pitched because of the soft, swaying movement of the image, the ball appearing from the bottom of the screen.

The child repositions the bat and drops it. He stares down at the bat, then covers his face, as if this were the worst failure one might ever know in life. And this reminds you of all the failing you've done. Even a successful life, like yours, could be charted by connecting the endless stream of failures. It might look like a nautical map, with deep blue showing the bigger losses and humiliations.

Ate you, says the image of the child.

I hate you, you decipher, *I hate you.*

For an instant, the camera moves into close-up, you think, but then you realize Robert is walking toward the boy.

Pick up the bat, he says.

The boy begins running. He trips. The camera keeps shooting.

[cut to: feet, legs, feet, dirt . . .]

Look, I haven't got time for this. Pick up the bat . . .

[cut to: black]

You consider the tone of Robert's last statement. It wasn't malicious, exactly, or even menacing, but really just exasperated—a man fed up with the pressures of a difficult child.

Your friend takes this break as an opportunity to escape, which the two of you will joke about later, and says that you've got to get going, actually, that the two of you have quite a long drive back to the city. And that's all your friend says. No outrage. No minor activism. No deep reading of the film or discussion of how the blunt images seemed, to you at least, nearly . . . unreal.

If it were *my* family, you think . . .

And here begins the breakup of the relationship you haven't even begun. In the film of the child. In yourself. In the coldness you now suspect in your friend.

The two of you will fight in the car on the way back to the city and it will be your first fight (you haven't even disagreed yet), and later you will make love for the first time. And the lovemaking will be very good because of the energy produced from the anger and verbally inflicted injuries, which will still be reverberating in the air like an echo. This first lovemaking will also contain the element of regret and the intent of healing with soft touches and flesh against flesh—which will corroborate your notion that you're normal.

But first comes the fight. In the car, you won't mention the film. It will seem too sad and sick and dangerous, too obvious, to even bring up. So the fight will be under the guise of jealousy. It will pertain to something about an ex-lover who keeps turning up in all the right or wrong places (depending on perspective) around the city—restaurants, bookstores, bars, coffeehouses—precisely when the two of you go to these places. The fight tonight in the car on the way back to the city will get nasty and personal, but it won't be nearly as bad as the fights you will have later. Those will get ugly.

The later fights will get ugly because the two of you will know that the end is coming, and with every insult, every long cold silence and refusal to touch, will be the attitude of let's just get it over with, the understanding that cruelty might speed up the process. (It will.) But even then there will be a part of you that feels compelled to hold on, that will

remember all the physical and mental and emotional invest-
ments that connect the two of you.

And sex, of course, will be the hardest of these invest-
ments to finally give up. Because despite everything that's
coming, the sex will, for the most part, be good on a bad day
and toe-curling, wake-up-the-neighbors great on a good day.
Sex. The mere mention of the word will arouse you. And this
wonderful and sad fucking will exacerbate the pain (but in a
way that is not entirely negative).

However, things will be great, for a while, as they usually are in something worth calling a relationship. And you
will tell people, lots of people, how great things are, which
will make the end, the explaining and re-explaining of why it
didn't work, even more depressing and humiliating.

But first, not far from the now of this story, during the
great time, you will invest yourself completely, give yourself over to this lover's fantasies with unencumbered trust.
And vice versa. And one of these fantasies—not yours—will
involve a palm-sized camcorder, a close relative of the 16 mm
camera that Robert is packing up now. You will always
worry about the videotape of the two of you appearing somewhere, tangled together and grunting in a way you will find
unsettling, actually kind of sad and wonderful like those last
parting fucks will be. The audio of the tape will be filled with
your moaning and expletives and commands and you'll think:
Damn, do I sound like that? I don't sound like that.

You will imagine yourself naked on television screens
in hospital waiting rooms and up in the corners of bars as
tattooed men ogle you and joke about a blemish on your

ass. Your heart will speed up when you think of coin-operated TVs in old bus stations (are those still around?) and the small, blue screens hanging from the ceiling in the business-class section of an airplane. You will actually have a dream about watching yourself awkwardly fucking (performing a sort of anti-porn) on a wall of a thousand televisions like some moaning bug eye in the back of a Circuit City.

But all of this is much, much later.

Right now you are still trying to get out of your friend's family's house. Everyone is standing up, following the two of you toward the door, patting you on the back and saying how nice it was to meet you and that they hope you will come back and visit. And you will come back and visit because your relationship with your friend—which will begin just hours from now when you put your hand on the soft inner part of your friend's leg and say you're sorry and then make a self-deprecating joke as a prelude to the kiss that will *get things rolling*—will last for almost two years, if you count the last few months as on as opposed to off, which will be up for debate.

You stand at the door after shaking hands and want desperately to say something about the film of the child, even though there is no evidence with which to accuse anyone of anything, just vague, poorly captured images and a sinking feeling. You want your friend to say something, to stand up for the child, because your friend, when you get right down to it, is a bit smarter than you and a lot more articulate and able to point out not only the problem as it manifests itself in reality but also its *deeper cultural causes*.

To break the uncomfortable silence, you say it was nice meeting everyone. Another long silence, empty looks, head-nodding, frozen smiles.

That's it. You smile back. And you hate your smile. You are flooded with the vague energy of disgust, which you will sweat out later tonight as you bump knees and noses trying to *find a groove*.

Your soon-to-be lover already seems distant to you—before anything even happens, before you have even given each other pet names—like a negative of the person you've been wanting. You won't think of this moment as significant later, at the end. There will have been too many moments to consider by then, all containing their own amount of clarity and confusion, cause and effect. There will be no record, no rewind, no freeze-frame. It will vanish from your conscious-ness like a shadow in direct light, like a spent reel of film.

The family is smiling and waving. You are turning and walking down the driveway toward the car, holding your soon-to-be-lover's hand. The future spreads out in front of you. Streetlights hum. The night is black and cold. You stare ahead through your own breath.

A Stupid Story

K IDS LINED UP ALONG *the sidewalks. Shuffling in the cold. Under these factories. Smells like raw sewage. God, it's like they're knee-deep in their own crap. Smell that? No place to hang out, if you ask me. But what the hell do I know, right, old guy like me?*

Want one? Don't smoke? Fine. Suit yourself.

My boy Jimbo used to hang out here. His name was Jim, actually James, but I called him Jimbo since he was young. Used to be one of them, standing right down there all the time.

No, just a little farther up.

One time I picked up a kid right here. Right about here. Me and the wife had just had World War III. I merged over toward the kids, cutting across the left lane, to pull up along the curb like a regular, like someone out for a blow. Some bitch honked at me and shot the finger. If I was someone else, or maybe if it'd just been a few months earlier, I don't know, I might have blown her away. Seriously, I might have shot her. Bitch, know what I mean? Sure you do. You don't just go beeping and shooting the bird at people. What world do you live in, lady? People get shot. You wouldn't do that. Right? It's stupid. Exactly. Crazy. Down here, too. Yeah. (Laughter.) Dead in the sewage. (Laughter.) Dumb bitch.

Anyway, traffic was real bad that evening. Taillights here to there. Could smell gas in the car with you. Even though it was winter, windows rolled up, heat on. True story: Kid in my neighborhood goes to the hospital after falling asleep with a gas-soaked rag over his face, trying to get high. Same kid is now almost thirty, walks around town with a Walkman on, smiling. Walks like twenty miles a day. Still lives at home, in a room above the garage. Never had a job. True story. Swear to God. You ought to write that down.

That day I pulled up to the curb, and I caught a wheel on the sidewalk and then dropped off, making all the kids look. Some laughed. I felt a little stupid. I was kinda nervous. I'll give you that.

I rolled down my window.

Yeah, said a kid with those weird dreadlocks. Right, like that, like, I don't know, cigars or something. 'Bout yea long.

Anyway, Hi, I said. I pointed to the kid I'd seen before, a few days earlier. He was sitting against the fence, look-ing sort of lost, like Jimbo. He seemed perfect, like a stunt double, swear to God. He looked like someone who'd hang himself in a second. I said to the kid in my window, Him. I pointed. Over there, I said. Could you get him for me?

Kid turned and yelled, Beano! This guy wants you. He said "wants" like I was the world's biggest perv, spanking it in my car already.

Beano looked around, hesitated for a sec, then stood up and walked over to my window. His breath was like exhaust hissing out of his nose it was so cold. He had on a hooded sweatshirt and a hat on backward, Padres, or maybe Orioles. Black. I couldn't believe the resemblance. I couldn't believe it.

He goes, What?

I smiled. I couldn't believe it. I know, I said that. But I couldn't believe it. Just like Jimbo, my boy, with all this attitude.

I was wondering if you wanted to make a few bucks, I said.

Nah, man, I ain't like that, he said. Those kids are down there—he pointed behind me—on the next corner.

It'll take about an hour, I said. I'll give you fifty bucks, I said. I showed him a crisp fifty, like this. Nothing sexual, I said. That ain't me, weird sex stuff with kids. And it ain't right.

What then? he goes.

Get in and we'll talk, I said. You won't have to do anything.

Right, man, he said. You'll try to eat my eyeballs or something, Mr. Dahmer.

That's what he called me, Mr. Dahmer.

Fifty bucks, I said. And I ain't going to touch you. I was real stern, real serious about that. I ain't a perv. You know

that. You can see that. I'm fifty. I gotta good job. I gotta wife.
I pay taxes, a registered Republican. I don't go for boys. You
write that down, you put that in there. Don't set up your
story to lead people to believe something, you know.

I don't know, he goes. He looked around.

Fifty. I held up the bill again, like this.

You touch me, you make a move, and you'll be sorry.
My dad's a cop.

I go, Hey, I won't lay a hand on you.

Seriously, he goes, pointing at me, getting in, if I say the
word, you let me out.

We drove to St. Anne's. I was thinking about Jimbo. I was
sweating a little under my arms. Just a little bit, even though
it was cold. He kinda gave me the creeps. Sitting there. I'm
not going to lie. I was thinking about my boy, my son, and
getting pretty sad but I didn't want this new kid, Beano, to
know I was sad so I put on the radio station Jimbo used to
like, I mean back when he would talk to me, and pushed in
the lighter and lit a smoke and offered Beano one, too. Want
one? No still, huh? Suit yourself. You like that station? I like
country. Old stuff. This? I don't know what the hell this is.
But, hey, you like it, I'll keep it on.

Anyway, Beano took the smoke and asked me what I
wanted from him.

I want you to be my son, I said, and later, you know,
when I started really thinking about all this, when I started
thinking that maybe it'd be nice to talk to someone about
this, I kept going back to the way I said that. I mean, I'm not

trying to get all sappy or anything but that's just a weird way to put it, you know.

I'm like the next guy. I ain't immune to stuff. I feel things.

What? Beano goes.

Act like my son, I go.

You mean pretend to be your son? Beano goes.

Yeah. Is it that complicated? Fifty bucks. Half an hour. No big deal.

For what?

What?

What do you want me to pretend I'm your son for?

His grandma. My wife's mother. She loved my son Jimbo. She always asks about him. My wife already told her, but she's, you know, out of it. She's old and half crazy. She won't remember. She can't remember one minute to the next.

See, I guess I thought I was going to be a hero. I felt like I needed to do something nice—for me, for Nana, for Jimbo, even for my wife maybe. I don't know. Why am I talking about this shit? You ever feel like that, like you need to do something decent? I grew up real religious. Baptist. Don't mess with a Baptist, man. Christ. Fire and brimstone. Satan just like embedded in the particles in the air or something. You should put down that I'm religious. Because I am. I love God plenty. I ask him stuff sometimes. Like, Hey, God, how did everything get so fucked up?

Wait a minute, Beano goes. Jimbo's dead?

Nah nah, I said. I paused. I got kinda, I don't know, you know, like, some kind of, I don't know. Nothing like that, I said, he's just . . . unavailable.

But if your wife already told the old lady, maybe it ain't such a good idea.

You want the money or no? I say.

We were almost there at that point, a few blocks from here; know where it is? Right.

Beano looked out the window. Headlights were bright in the side view mirror, which was right below his chin from this angle. I was looking like this. He was sitting right there, where you are.

Real quiet he goes, Yeah, I want the money. Just saying.

I lit another cigarette, asked if he wanted one. No. Don't worry. I ain't going to ask you again.

Then he goes, right out of the blue, You divorced?

None of your business, I said. Then: No, I ain't divorced. I said I was married, didn't I?

All right, man. Not like I care. Just seems like you're probably divorced. Seems like you live alone, is all.

I'm married, I said, like I told you. For now. Then I fig- ured I didn't owe this kid an explanation. I said, Things are just a little weird. Me and my wife have a lot on our minds.

He looked over at me. Yeah, he said. Just pay me my fifty like you promised.

St. Anne's. You can never find a parking space. I drive laps. Laps. It gives me a headache every time I come, if you want to know.

Nana, my wife's mother, who was really like my one and only mother during the whole early part of our marriage, before she had a stroke and then all the complications and then just got all old and senile and incoherent, was up on the fifth floor, in a private room that was costing my wife and me our whole retirement. When it rains it pours, know what I mean? That could be your title. When It Rains It Pours. Or: John Barclay: Everything He Touches Turns to Shit. Or: John's Shit World.

Me and Beano got on the elevator and went up and didn't say anything the whole way. He fidgeted just like Jimbo. I wondered if he took anything, any medications; I wondered what he thought about, if he thought, you know, bad stuff, sad stuff, whatever, I don't know. But I didn't ask because I wanted this to be as simple as possible.

Now I'm not even going to get into the stuff about Nana, tell you about the machines and her expressions and the bedpans and the sour smell of dying people, and so on. It's depressing. Depressing. Horrible is what it is. Life. Christ. I don't know. Jesus. Push in the lighter there. Satan in air particles. What about that? (Laughs, uncomfortably.)

I can't save people from what goes on in their heads and make their lives right. I mean, what am I? I'm a kid's dad and I'm supposed to be able to fix his whole life. He wouldn't even talk to me. I'm supposed to make my wife want to dance. What? What am I? What am I? Who the fuck am I? I'm this old guy. I got a job. I got stuff to do. Work. I wish I could change things. I'd fix everything, I'd fix everybody, I swear *to God, I would, I'd do it. I'd save my marriage, make time move backward. If I could, I'd erase whole years and then do it all over again, but prepared this time, tuned in to the little stuff I missed the first time. My life ain't peachy. You don't see me hanging myself in a shed. That's just selfish, if you ask me, that's just trying to hurt the people who love you and make them feel guilty is all.*

All right. Sorry. I'm rambling. Keep that up and I might start to look really bad, huh?

So Beano sat in Nana's room and I told Nana that Beano was my son Jimbo. Jimbo was doing really great in school. He was probably going to go to college. He was on the debate team, football, all kinds of bullshit.

I whispered to Beano to tell Nana that he loved her. Why not? Jimbo maybe would have. I doubt it. But maybe. Fifty, I whispered.

I love you, Nana, Beano said, but he was looking at me and he was turning a little pink. He didn't sound convincing.

I pointed at her and gave him a face like, Come on. He leaned over her then, like he really meant it, and said, real sincere, too, Nana, I love you. This kid. I didn't know him from anyone. I wondered who he said that to for real. If anyone. I got that kind of mind, you know. I wonder what people are thinking, what they might say if given the opportunity. Some people say I'm pretty philosophical.

She said, Oh I love you, too, Jim. You're my best boy. You're my baby, my little chubby baby. Nana loves her Jim.

Her face is all wrinkled but God it was, well, it was something. Nearly killed me, kid. That one nearly took me out.

Then a few other things happened—a nurse came in, I turned on the TV and me and Beano and Nana watched Wheel of Fortune. One of the puzzles was COOKIES IN THE COOKIE JAR; another was GOODBYE BLUE SKY. I got both right away, before the Amway rep from Syracuse or the teacher or whatever from Phoenix or Philadelphia or Fargo. Then we left. That was basically it.

So I brought Beano back down here. I gave him the fifty and he got out. We didn't say anything. A deal's a deal in my book. I promise, I deliver.

Then Beano stopped on the sidewalk and turned and looked at me like he wanted to say something.

I rolled down the window.

He looked at his shoes, scuffed something on the concrete. He was a nervous kid.

He goes, I'm sorry about your son, man.

I didn't say anything. He looked at me. I nodded.

He walked off. I drove home.

I don't know. It's a stupid story, isn't it? I don't think this means anything. But if you polish it up, maybe.

This is really just something I tell people sometimes. Not like I dwell on it. This is just a story I tell people. You know, to talk.

Gray World

LISTEN: LOCKED AWAY, he began his education. He had time now to learn, after years of avoiding it. It was written in the letters I never answered. He was full of knowledge.

He learned math in a classroom the color of slate, chalk squeaking out numbers and signs on a blackboard. An old man, an inmate, a man who did something illegal to his own children long ago, sweated and talked about theorems, formulas. Numbers, in the abstract, he found difficult. The old man, he wrote, was smart but a bad teacher, full of water and ideas and terrible secrets, unable to fully share even mathematics for fear of revealing a dark part of himself. He worked hard, though—to learn, to understand all the basic things he'd ignored throughout his life, to prove something. At lunch he counted men the way children count apples or spotted cartoon dogs. He learned that two men were most likely able to overpower one, that three men could always overpower one, no matter what you might hear, and that it was better to be one of the three than the only one.

In wood shop he made a clock, a battery-run, working clock he was proud of, that someone smashed when he wasn't looking. Then he made a shiv out of a thin piece of PVC pipe and electrical tape for when he found out who smashed his clock, which, I believe, had come to symbolize, in some vague way to him, his progress as a human being, his ability to do things people on the outside might consider productive. He needed to kill the fucker who crushed his human progress. He stabbed someone he didn't like, hoping that he was the crusher of human progress. But it was the wrong man. Inside, these things happen. All is flux. The right man and the wrong man are the same man; it's all about intention and revenge, the means not the end. Someone deserves it; someone gets it; if they're not the same someone, who really gives a fuck? For this he slept in a dark room for forty-five days, until his eyes were glued shut and his lips were cracked and his skin was the color of the squeaking chalk the old man used for the theorems. He counted the days in cold, soupy meals.

In the letters he misspelled the crucial words. He spelled "niggers" with one *g* and "spicks" with an *x*. I found myself fixing some of his letters before putting them away— an old habit. P.S., he wrote, please write me back. Please. Loneliness is the worst disease, because it is survivable. He used the word "please" like a weapon. I had hated him the way you can only hate someone you love.

He learned quickly that blacks hated whites and whites hated blacks. A fact, like natural law. There was no

compromise. A compromise would get the white compro-
miser killed by the rest of the whites. The same was true
for the blacks. Hispanics, however, were different; depending on their skin tone they could go, occasionally, either
way, if they knew the right people, although mostly they
stuck together, too. It was different in the West, he had
heard, where there were more Hispanics. But in Virginia,
he wrote, the spix are few and can go either way. Many
didn't even speak English. Inside, he wrote, it would not
be bad to be light brown. It would not be bad to not know
the language, which was a language of senselessness and
violence and ruin. He longed, I imagine, to be unidentified,
lost, invisible.

He also learned, slowly, to read and write. Just a few
years ago. In his thirties. Then came the letters, in a killing
flood. He wrote all the time, to me, an old girlfriend, his
mother, filling up our desk drawers, boxes. He wrote and
wrote and wrote, manic with the power of language, roam-
ing back and forth through his whole life, remembering, in-
venting, reinventing, shaping, trying to articulate, looking . . .
He read the Bible. It was the only book they'd give him; it
was the only title he could remember. It took him a long time
to read it, but he found it both cryptic and intoxicating. So
he read it again—and again and again . . . Later, he felt God
in his fingertips and was sorry for so many things that he
could not stop crying. He lived in a sorrow you can only find
in a dark place without freedom, a place where time meant
everything and nothing and space was a myth passed around
for comfort.

He learned that Jesus Christ was crucified for our sins and that on the third day he rose from the dead. He liked that, rising from the dead. He liked the idea of Heaven, he wrote me, of just dropping your body and moving on. He liked that the end of the Bible became dark and cautionary— a bad dream, a bad trip—warning of a preordained end to us all. He said he liked St. John as much as Jesus, maybe more. He said he knew Judas, and Paul, and that Job, an ex–auto mechanic, constantly paced around, beating on his bars. The Bible made him feel small. It was so big, so beyond him. He professed his love for God, which helped, but only some. This introduced an immensity, in the face of which he felt himself shrinking. He had been an empty vessel up to now, he wrote, misspelling the words, and now he was ashamed.

As a Christian, after learning about the death of the body, of all bodies, he did not so much mind the things he did. He had learned early on that it was best to choose—as much as one was able to choose—a group of men who you did not mind having sex with. This way, he learned, sex was paid for by protection from others who might want to have sex with you. He learned to give himself to a few to be saved from the many—he thought of this in instinctive mathematical terms. He learned that he was probably not a homosexual but was capable, in certain circumstances, of acting convincingly as one. He learned, early, that being raped was a terrible, violent, humiliating thing but that fighting it often made it worse; fighting it made it all violence and no sex; pretending was the way to go; pretending was self-preservation, a saving of skin.

He prayed every night. His asshole bled. He never got an erection again, never, he wrote, even when he fantasized about women, the ones that seemed almost fake, the ones from magazines with giant breasts and white-blonde hair, those plastic female Americans that went about making themselves for the sole purpose of fucking, the ones that used to work for him every time, the ones that now turned into smiling men right there in the middle of his head. He had become, he wrote, a woman, a whore. I am becoming plastic.

He cursed God and then apologized. He bit his lip, tasted blood, thought, *I am still real. I am still here.* It wasn't him they wanted to destroy, he reasoned, staring at a ceiling that was the same cold color as everything else; it was his body, and the body, he had learned from Jesus Christ Himself, was temporary.

He learned, then, to cooperate, sacrifice.

He learned from a priest, the same man who helped him to read, that having killed another human being (pointlessly and intentionally) considerably lessened his chances of being saved. It doesn't just happen, the priest told him, you have to work. His last letters are about the difficulty of being saved.

He needed to work harder than he could.

His body was so tired.

He learned, when he was exhausted, that drinking cleaning fluid was not good enough, that they could pump your stomach, bring everything up in a blue stream. He learned that it was hard to leave your body in here if they didn't want you to.

You did not own your body in prison. Nothing belonged to you. Nothing had worth. You were plastic and you could be melted down for materials.

Please, he wrote me, please write back.

I own boxes full of pleading. I own a man's heart in pencil marks.

He learned that a belt, even if you could get one, was not the best thing; buckles are made of different pieces, and different pieces, as a rule, eventually come apart. Every little thing is solitary, ultimately.

The last thing he read: the soul is light, infinite, and always glowing; the body, this life, a burden.

Intersections
(DOWNTOWN RICHMOND, VIRGINIA,
JUNE 1st, 1994)

URBAN RENEWAL IS RIPPING the cracked and with-ered face off of downtown. Jackhammers and big orange signs. Dump trucks and workers loitering in intersections. Someone was elected (the bus driver looking through his vertical, convex window at the rutted street below can't remember who) on the promise of a new face, a makeover for this sagging section of city. Right, thinks the driver. Just picture it: spit shined and sparkling. Pinch and tuck and tighten. Put up new signs, cut taxes, offer some kind of small business loan to anyone daring to open a shop. Make the cops move downtown and have cookouts with the crackheads. He's a bus driver, drives these streets every day, knows this town from the inside, this bus like a blood cell cruising the pocked, asphalt veins; he knows. Knows better, is what. You can do what you want—legislate, promise, procrastinate, lie.

Probably doesn't much matter. But damn, how about fixing the potholes?

The bus driver (African American, 46, 6' 1", 227 pounds and on a diet because of prodding from his wife, stomach rumbling *at this very moment* and nothing in his lunch box but carrots and rice cakes) has driven this road, crossed and recrossed this grid of city blocks—not far from where he grew up—four times a day, five days a week, for fifteen years. Not a bad job, driving. All right, maybe it's a good job—benefits, decent salary, retirement plan, the whole bit. Of course he'd quit if he could, sure. It's a job, not a career. Got to feed the family, got to make the bucks, but that's not what fills your heart, man. No, not exactly for the soul, this job, but not bad for the soul either, that's not what he means, just, you know, *soulless,* he thinks, coming to the seventh stop along his morning route, air brakes doing that *squeak whoosh squeak ssss* he knows so well, hears sometimes in his dreams. Singing. That's what he'd like to do—have someone pay him to belt out a tune that would turn you into a puddle of tears. Now church choir fills the heart, is good for the soul; watching his son play baseball, how he can knock that ball into space; and his daughter, too, bringing home straight-A report cards—that's the stuff, family—his wife's liquid eyes, her silky hair, the curve of her sweet-smelling neck where he likes to softly place his lips, so softly. He likes going home at the end of the day and not thinking about a big machine: engine going like a sick cow, gears popping, stony faces floating in his mirror. And the hemorrhoids—don't even get him started on the hemorrhoids! Let's say he won the lottery—*if*

I won the lottery—won maybe a modest ten million, which works out to be about five hundred grand a year. First thing he'd do, after vomiting on his shiny standard-issue black shoes, would be to quit. Not even pick up his last check. Say to the boss, *Keep it, buy yourself something nice.* Then he'd get his family, light of his life, three human beings he loves so much that sometimes just thinking about them brings tears to his eyes, everything they wanted. New car, new baseball equipment, new teachers, new schools (his daughter makes straight A's in a school with metal detectors and a couple of murders a year, so many assaults that the school board had to get tougher on how they defined "assault"). And at his seventh stop (a stop he has made approximately fifteen thousand times in the last fifteen years), as the door accordions open with a mechanical sigh, as he lets on the street preacher who smells of rancid meat and urine, smells of rummaged-through restaurant Dumpsters and puddles of pickled wino piss, he knows that, with that cool ten mil, he'd move as far from this place as possible.

The preacher (an emaciated guy with a matted red beard and long hair the color of soot) steps left right left up the bus stairs, knowing that right left right will hurl the universe spinning toward a disaster. (Every day he gets on at the bus driver's seventh stop and rides six blocks, gets off then to walk six blocks, then rides a final six blocks to a place where he stands and attempts, loudly, to untangle the infinitely intricate puzzle of the last days on Earth: These Days. He repeats this pattern at the end of the day exactly backward, always taking the steps left right left to keep the universe

from spinning toward a premature disaster; he's got enough
to think about without that on his head.) Preacher likes the
bus. Comfortable. Gives him time to read, think, make notes
in the margins of his Bible on top of layers of other notes.
(He's been thinking about good and evil for more years even
than the black bus driver, whose name he does not know,
has been driving this bus. He graduated from a prestigious
Southern university twenty-five years ago. And then, certain
moderately concerned people said, *he just lost it*. He doesn't
remember those people—friends, lovers, teammates, roommates, colleagues—the people who said things like *just lost
it,* although occasionally one will show up, make a brief
cameo in a dream. They often have fangs and spit like exotic
poisonous snakes.) He's devised some theories. Considers,
now, a couple of Psalms—singsongy, poetic, they burn his
fingers when he touches the words. Good and evil exist together in the world, in each of us, mixed, or, no, that's not
what he means, not mixed, but on top of one another, yes,
oil and water, in the same murky puddle, the puddle being
us. It's the comfortable same, the bus (there is divine peace
in routine; protective angels live in the familiar movement,
the practiced gesture): same time, same faces, same route and
scenery, same flesh and metal smells, same drone and squeak
of engine and seat, same soft sibilant sounds of quiet talk:
whisper whisper whisper whisper, keep it all to yourself, put
a lid on it, shake it up, motherfuckers, whores, cunts. He
knows what they're saying, God knows what they're saying, and not saying, those little secrets like rotting teeth in
their mouths, what they take to bed with them and wouldn't

breathe out, wouldn't let foul the air, even in the dark. Same everything. Same every day. A leaning hotel, a beautiful woman, a shiny car, a packed diner with glass skin. A store, a group of boys (baggy pants, expensive shoes, cigarettes), bicycles. Streetlights, a corner, an alley, an empty lot where weeds strive from the cracks in the concrete. Good and evil, love and hate, weeds and concrete, the same murky puddle—us. (Notes on top of notes.) Empty lot gets him thinking (gets him scrawling like a polygraph—lie lie lie!), feeling the crackle and pulse up his spine. A bum was found there, a guy he sort of knew, bound in electrical tape and beaten deader than dead, dirt and trash and cigarette butts stuffed into his mouth, tiny red burns covering his face and neck and scalp and hands. Covering his hands like stigmata. People heard things, television said, but people always hear things. Lambs. A stop. Man gets on. Woman gets on. Child gets on, a girl. Seat beside the preacher's empty. They know who he is. He's got their number. He reads their dreams like delicate scrolls. Good and evil, oil and water, same murky puddle, us, weeds and concrete, dirt in his mouth, tiny red wounds. Driver looks at him, big black guy with the glare in his eye who thinks he knows God because he hangs a cross from the mirror, because he bows his head and gets herded into church Sundays like an idiot beast for slaughter. Black guy looks at him in the mirror, looks, cheap cross swinging like a dog dick. *Religion is pounds of flesh and bottles of blood, brother,* he wants to shout. *If I were as weak a Christian as you, I'd divorce myself from life* (he read that somewhere). Doesn't speak, though; chews his fingernails instead. Six stops later, gets up, takes his bag and Bible. People turn, look, know who he is, know he can save them or destroy them with the tiniest beat of his heart. *I forgive you,* he says to the driver (as he does every day). *Thanks,* says the driver (as he does every day at the thirteenth stop). Door sighs its tired sigh. Preacher gets off, left right left (to walk the six blocks). Day unreels. Skyline blurs. Lamps hang their heads. Good and evil, oil and water, the same murky puddle.

Girl catches an elbow in the biceps. Big mouthful of that stench before she can speak, like a dead animal, that smell, fresh and dead, entrails still on the road, or like that guy in the VA hospital where she volunteered when she was a teenager, the big one with like fungus or mold growing under the folds of his breasts, maggots in there before he was even dead, like that, something dead or dying. *I'm sorry, Miss, forgive me,* says the old guy. (The preacher spends sleepless days and nights at a time pondering religious notions of forgiveness.) Backing away, feeling the pinch and pucker of her face, muscles cinching up in the stink, and taking a long, deep whiff anyway. *I forgive you,* she says, walking on, stepping away, breathing in deep the air away from him, the clear, perfect air, rubbing her shoulder where she knows a bruise will form (she bruises easily). I forgive you, she thinks, what a weird thing to say, even to a rotting homeless guy. Ought to say that to her mom. Yeah. Walks on, heading for the store. To get Velveeta cheese and pasta shells; two bucks and you have lunch and plenty left for dinner; or maybe just soup and a loaf of bread, the good wheat kind with the chunky little grains in the crust, probably not even real grains, sawdust or

something, just decoration, but still, good stuff, good deco-
rative stuff. Guy almost broke her arm, that's for sure. She
needs a sling or something, an ice pack. *I forgive you.* What
would Mom say to that? I forgive you for not understanding
graduate school, for not even being interested in painting, for
making her talk about things that don't interest her so they
can still do the mother-daughter chat. She loves her mom,
even if she drones on about her father working all the time,
and playing golf on the weekends, and never being interested
in sex, or at least rarely. Always wants to lay some heavy stuff
on her about sex and an older woman's needs, all tinged with
that New Age stuff she reads. Mom says that most women
find cunnilingus an arousing form of foreplay and a way to
become functionally more lubricated, *especially as you get
older.* Her father used to be into that sort of thing, *used to
be a real muff-diver.* He never went down on her anymore.
Always, at some point in the conversation, Mom makes it
around to her leaving this part of the city. Every time. From
uncomfortable sex talk with the woman who breast-fed her,
changed her diapers, put her hair in pigtails, told her how
pretty she was after she got dumped, to what a bad idea it
is to live in the city and go to that school, and how there is
bad energy in the "economically challenged" parts of cities.
Wishes she could explain, in one coherent breath, explain
how it's important to her to understand deep aesthetic theories of painting and art, and to know the history and progres-
sion and movements of art, understand that art is, as she once
read somewhere, a finite sphere and how the artist, the serious
artist, must know, in her own particular way, that sphere and

then hope and work and sweat to create something that can survive on the outer edge of that sphere and, hopefully, make that sphere grow as it must. Art. Spheres. That's what she's thinking about at this very moment as she walks. Spheres. Making a living is sort of beside the point. It's teleologically bohemian rather than professional. Can't say something that stupid and pretentious to her mother, after trudging through the whole cunnilingus spiel. Damn frustrating: She's sensitive to the desperate condition we humans find ourselves in. Wants to be an artist more than anything. Doesn't want to *sound* like she wants to be one. Wants to sound like she just naturally is one. Very cool. Very understated. The kind of artist people are always going on and on about but also the kind that never, ever, never wants to talk about her own work, its complexity, its depth. Aloof. Mysterious. Yeah. She gets trapped in this circular stuff, trapped thinking in grand arching metaphors and trying to get her mind around big thoughts. Or maybe they're really really small thoughts. She doesn't know. But she's not leaving. That's for sure. (Later, if she becomes that artist she hopes to become, she may attempt to dispense with the intellectual pretensions and find an honest, earnest, centered place from which to work and incorporate into her art everything she has ever known and felt, a much harder task, which may drive her to feelings of failure and futility, to stiff drink and thoughts of suicide.) Her work has improved in the city. She sees it in the brush stroke, the poetry of one motion leading to the next, feels it in her formal control. Her vision, whatever that means, has broadened and deepened. She knows this. Sure, she's become more aloof and meditative, like her mom says, like her friends say, more brooding and temperamental—all those clichés are true. And she reads too much, looks at paintings too much. But she's doing her best work. Like her new painting, *The Rape,* in which a girl walks to a corner store, like she is doing now, as two men, decently dressed, nonchalant, whisper behind her back. Best thing she's ever done. A year ago, *The Rape* would have been more overt, less evocative and subtle and dangerous (here is her nascent art vocabulary), without angry brush strokes suggesting menace in the calmness of the scene. No, in that big house outside of D.C., she would have shown the rape explicitly, blood and gore and ripped clothing, or with painfully bald metaphor—the men would have had dicks for noses and chubby little dick fingers holding thin, burning dick cigarettes—she would have lost everything, bored herself. Violence, orgasmic, finalized violence, has become passé. Not life. Life is scary. But she doesn't want to be clumsy, or obvious, isn't even interested in being accessible or commercially viable. She wants, instead, to be deep, to be subtle, like Woolf and James and Rhys and Joyce (she was an English major)—like that, art like a perfect little dream, all interior, all suggestion, all implicit. She walks; she strides. Her painting, in a certain way—in its intention, at least—is probably better than Caravaggio's painting of the same name, which focuses on a perpetrator, evokes empathy for all those driven to steal another's soul while desecrating the body (she read that somewhere). Her painting evokes sympathy for all involved, for the tragedy of living in a world full of fear, for perpetrators and victims, for the forces that make people either one or the other. All these men around here, dirty, lost men looking her over. She gets the creeps, paces around her apartment at night, rechecks the window locks, the dead bolt on the door, keeps a couple of lights on all the time, a phone by the bed. *The Rape* is a painting in which she faces her fear, tries it on like a comfortable pair of jeans, a painting in which every brush stroke contains a terrible sadness and beauty, a painting full of the sounds of distant gunshots and sirens and drunks and careless, broken people chattering in her mind. A painting as calm and dangerous as downtown at sunrise or dusk. Walking into the store, smiling at the clerk, she is thinking these things—how being here and watching people and the feeling of danger and low-wattage rage that lives in the concrete and steel and mortar and blank faces have given her something she didn't have before. *I'm scared to death, Mom,* she will say, *I'm so alive here that every scene, every tableau, every defeated glance, reminds me of death.* And I've never been worse. And I've never been better. And I forgive you for things you've never thought about.

She gets some food, just a can of soup. Lost her appetite on the way. (This happens when she really gets to thinking.) Pulls a wadded-up five from her jeans. Hands it to the clerk. He unfolds it and, holding it in both hands, rubs it back and forth along the edge of the counter to straighten it before giving the girl her change. Attractive girl. He's seen her a few times. Probably stuck up, like the rest of them. The clerk doesn't, as a rule, talk to the grad students around here, with their little beatnik glasses and requests for over-priced wines, with their big talk and expensive clothes made to look worn-out. Closes the cash register (smiling, falsely, at the young artist he doesn't know is an artist). Construction is killing him. That's the thing, or one of the things (one of the things that makes him the cruel, sad person he is). No one can even get down here, unless they come from the east. The people with the money come from the west. Two dollars and twenty-nine cents in three hours. His whole life has been a constant worry over money (he often says these exact words to his wife), over crumpled fives and inventory and big chain groceries just blocks away that can afford to buy and sell everything and especially the kids from this neighborhood who come in here and steal him blind. The money he makes from the old guys, he tells his wife (the yellow-eyed men buying Thunderbird and Mad Dog 20/20 and quarts of malt liquor and lottery tickets), he loses to the little thieves. These kids, these little fatherless, twenty-siblinged kids. Little thieves, bred to take and take. Welfare turns women into Chia Moms—just add water, or better yet wine, and they drop a litter, swear to God. These kids. Kids everywhere. Like the one he notices as the smiling grad student leaves (thinking those grand, depressing elliptical thoughts about art and life that he will never talk to her about). Like that kid, the black one with braids or locks or whatever the hell these people call this hairstyle. Walking around like he owns the place, picking things up, putting them down, labels facing backward, upside down, he doesn't care. None of them do. Watches the kid, maybe, what, fifteen, sixteen, ought to be in school in the middle of the day, as he picks up and puts down, opens coolers, wasting expensive cold air. Strutting, browsing, probably doesn't even have any money. *You going to buy something or not,* he says loudly.

Kid looks at him. Me, kid thinks. Walked in here a minute ago, maybe two. Been wondering about the white girl, the one that walks around talking to herself like she doesn't know it's dangerous around here, walks around at night. Walked in here with half a mind to tell her she needs to be more careful. Knows, though, that a black kid walking up to a white girl, a student, saying how she ought to stay in at night, be careful, wouldn't look right, might spook her more than it helps. (And now he's looking at the clerk framed there behind the counter by two video monitors, one for outside, one for inside.) TVs behind the clerk like a pair of eyes. Sees himself, a black wavering line in the middle of the left eye; sees himself seeing himself (a preconvicted criminal living on tape). *Yeah, I'm going to buy something. Is there a time limit for black people?* Fuck this old guy, looking at him like a thief, watching the nigger like a hawk because all niggers steal, fuck him (he, the kid, has stolen, in his entire lifetime, a Schwinn bicycle on a dare, several of his sisters' bras to play a joke on a friend, and numerous candy bars). Ought to steal something. Old motherfucker. Ought to round up all his brothers, a whole mess of scary black folk to hurl fried chicken and watermelon and curl activator and crack vials at your window, racist motherfucker. *Sign says no loitering,* says the old clerk. *Buy something or leave.* Says it real slow, like for a stupid person. Kid can't believe it, gets treated like a criminal in his own neighborhood because he doesn't have his hands in the air and his pockets turned inside out. He wouldn't give this man a penny, wouldn't piss on him if he was on fire. Cool, composed, kid says he doesn't see anything he wants, puts his hands up. (And it is only as he walks out, as he puts his hand on the thick glass of the door, leaving five perfect fingerprints, and the man says something under his breath, that the anger, those hard little bubbles of hate in his throat and in the pit of his stomach, take over.) Puts his hand on the unsteady magazine rack by the door, yanks it (one small act of aggression and release, almost thoughtless, the slightest twitch of the arm; and *right now,* elsewhere in the city, other acts of aggression, both small and large, misdemeanors and felonies, just and unjust, random and premeditated, are also happening). Spills the metal and the magazines along the floor, glossy covers sliding over the greasy white tiles behind him. *Club, Hustler, Penthouse, Vibe, Ebony.* Kid wants to slap the old man in the face like some whiny, spoiled child. But he is in a flat-footed sprint down the block already. Knows better than not to run, knows he needs to get down one of these alleys and out on another street because a nigger running around this neighborhood will be picked up sure as shit. Turns the corner onto Main (having no idea that it is the next leg of the bus driver's route), legs pumping, and hits the big white woman like he's hitting a brick wall. Puts her large and hard on her ass. Watches her bounce.

Woman feels a small rock embedded in her right butt cheek. No pain yet, just numbness, shock. Kid says *sorry,* kid says *sorry oh my god let me help you up,* kid says, *you okay, you all right,* and is gone, sprinting, bobbing and weaving along the crowded sidewalk, shouting as he goes, *Really sorry!* This has been her day. (If this were six months later and she was taking that night class at the university in an effort to become a matriculated student at the age of thirty-four, she would say that this incident was a physical manifestation/representation of the crappiness of her first day in the city. She does not, however, think or say this now.) Standing up, she counts to ten as people step around her. I'm fine, she thinks, looking up, thanks everyone for not stepping on my face. She counts. Counting calms her down, an effortless sort of meditation (it's how she keeps from hitting her daughter sometimes, counting). Keeps her from yelling what's what at that goddamn black kid. (She moved in with her sister last night, into a loft just a few blocks away, so she could find a job here, because she lost her job of six years at home and figured the city was the best place to come to find a good job. So far she's filled out five applications, two for waitress positions, and been flat turned away at three other places—and then she gets knocked down walking to the bus stop.) Eight . . . nine . . . ten. This has been her day. Remembers her two-year-old daughter throwing food all over her sister's kitchen this morning. Almost threw it back; she wanted, she ached, to dump the whole mushy meal over her daughter's head (she can't believe how hard it is to be a mother). She would have done it maybe if her sister wasn't there. Walked off, though, counting. Looked in the bathroom mirror. Thought how she wouldn't hire herself because she just wasn't pretty enough, and so fat. Fat fat fat. Then she thought of her daughter. Then she thought of wanting to dump food on her, how cathartic that would be. How evil that is. How beautiful her daughter is, just a baby. How she doesn't know better. Remembers, now, how she sat on her sister's toilet with her insides just a churning mess because she was nervous about the job stuff, bawling like a child as her daughter sat in the other room rubbing food all over her face, cooing that puzzled, beautiful little coo. This has been her day. Guy a block over, preaching and screaming into the crowd, some kind of Bible in his hand with writing all over it, looked right into her eyes while he was talking about sodomy and "vitriolic dykes." Big-boned, OK, short hair, OK, but not gay. Walking, side-stepping people on the sidewalks, she takes in the city, looks at it, breathes it, tastes it, how different it is from home, the hilly Virginia countryside. Everyone here has a blank face. (Her anger wanes, as if disappearing into the noise and odd-smelling air—hot asphalt on a southern breeze—and it is replaced by a funk, a deep, bone-chilling funk that anyone, if they were looking, could see take shape on her face.) She stands at the bus stop, afraid of sitting. Rock feels like it's still stuck in her skin. People are staring at her, staring at her back, seeing how huge she is, or whispering about her, the fat lady, the fat dyke who abuses her child, who doesn't love her beautiful child. Everyone, every face, is a chiseled stone, their expressions so rigid, the cold eyes afraid of betraying what's beneath, which could be anything: a killer, an angel, a fool, or just the shell of a human, like the husks of cicadas stuck to trees back home. (And her own face is like this as she looks, catches eyes, looks away, though she doesn't think about it.) Bus stops. *Squeak whoosh squeak ssss.* Bus driver swings open the door (he's still calculating his lottery winnings after taxes and setting up his extended family: his mother in a rest home, his brother in Georgia, his favorite uncle Donald, and so on). He stares right into her eyes and smiles and says, in a musical baritone, *Heeellloooo.* She smiles—*my bus driver sounds like Barry White*—wants to thank him, wants to tell him how he really saved her, how a hello at the right time is like water in the desert, which would be stupid and melodramatic, she realizes, especially here. (He is smiling because next stop he gets to take his lunch break and he's thinking about getting rid of the carrots and rice cakes and getting something *of substance,* but she doesn't know this, and takes it, the smiling, personally.) She sits in the seat nearest him, her eyes finding his in the mirror.

Imaginary Birds

(EXIT)

ONCE UPON A TIME, an old woman lived two doors down from a young writer, in a place where violence, of one degree or another, happened every day, a place where the young writer himself had been mugged for six dollars, where the leather-clad homosexual living above him had been beaten so badly that he had to be fed through a tube in his nose for a week, a place, in fact, where the old woman's son, the writer learned one day, had been murdered for no discernible reason while jogging in a park (he didn't have six dollars or his wallet with him, wasn't wearing a leather biker hat or chaps), and all this woman did now, as far as the writer could tell, was stand on her stoop, two doors down, which was in a line of stoops all basically identical except for the colors they were painted—stoops that dated back to Civil War reconstruction—and smile a crooked, left-veering smile because of age or perhaps a certain minor palsy

that had wrenched her face slightly to the right and frozen
it there, forcing her smile to kind of *head left,* just like that,
charmingly crooked, so when she spoke to people walking
by—anyone would do—she was always smiling with a beautifully deformed face when she said, *Hey you, there, young
man, do you hear that, do you hear those beautiful birds
singing their song,* and the young man, of course, who in this
particular instance was the writer and who, perhaps because
of a certain unwillingness to let himself go completely insane
just yet, didn't hear any birds—or it could have been because
of the very simple fact that there *were no birds* anywhere near
there, not real ones anyway, not even a pigeon, a filthy pigeon
trailing a line of gray-speckled shit across the statues of dead
people whose names had all been forgotten—but this young
man, the writer, stopped anyway and looked at the woman
and the woman looked at him, smiling, and he smiled back
and listened even harder but still all he heard was traffic and
a little wind and a distant car alarm screaming at itself, yet as
he stared at her, her bent, old, broken body, her hands like
gnarled roots, her long, white hair curled up on her head like,
he actually thought this, a small cat, he decided to play along
because he wasn't in any hurry, being unemployed and just
getting over a mild but to him still serious little problem with
his mind, so he said that he did hear them and he thought
maybe they were mockingbirds, and she said, *No no no,* they
weren't mockingbirds—*mockingbirds?* she said—but rather
songbirds that sang so beautifully that there wasn't even a
name for them yet, so there was no way to talk about them
at all, you just had to sit on the old stoop and smile and

listen closely and be very still and open yourself up to the song, and so the young writer—still staring with his mouth open—and the smiling old woman leaned close together on a street where it was not really safe, particularly after dark, which was on its way (falling, right now, down the face of dirty brick buildings), listening to a song by birds that were so beautiful that they didn't exist or have a name, and it was then, right then, at dusk, with the light a strange blue-purple, that the writer saw, in the back of the old woman's eyes, the tiny black reflections of birds wheeling about in the sky.

PHOTO BY AMY MILLER

GREG BOTTOMS is the author of two other books. His debut, *Angelhead: My Brother's Descent into Madness*, was an *Esquire* Book of the Year in 2000. Bottoms holds an MFA from the University of Virginia, where he was a Henry Hoyns Fellow, and has contributed to publications such as the *Believer, Bookforum, Salon, Oxford American*, and *Utne Reader*. He is currently an assistant professor of English at the University of Vermont.

Printed in the United States
by Baker & Taylor Publisher Services